ISBN 978-1-331-80439-0
PIBN 10236917

1 MONTH OF
FREE
READING

at

www.ForgottenBooks.com

By purchasing this book you are
eligible for one month membership to
ForgottenBooks.com, giving you
unlimited access to our entire
collection of over 1,000,000 titles via
our web site and mobile apps.

To claim your free month visit:

www.forgottenbooks.com/free236917

THE

LIFE OF JOHN THOMPSON,

A FUGITIVE SLAVE;

CONTAINING HIS HISTORY OF 25 YEARS IN BONDAGE, AND
HIS PROVIDENTIAL ESCAPE.

WRITTEN BY HIMSELF.

WORCESTER:
PUBLISHED BY JOHN THOMPSON.
MDCCCLVI.

---

*From the estate of
Margaret B. Wilson
Nov.*

WORCESTER:
PRINTED BY C. HAMILTON,
PALLADIUM OFFICE.

3/10/69 CS

PREFACE.

It would be an unprecedented act to send into the world a work of the magnitude of this volume, without a preface; and I am glad to avail myself of the opportunity, which custom not only allows but prescribes, to say something of the work before you. Its history is as follows: It was suggested to me about two years since, after relating to many the main facts relative to my bondage and escape to the land of freedom, that it would be a desirable thing to put these facts into permanent form. I first sought to discover what had been said by other partners in bondage once, but in freedom now, and from what States they came. I found many of my brethren from other and remote States, had written on the subject, but scarcely any from Maryland. I am aware that now, when public opinion makes it no martyrdom to denounce slavery, there are multitudes of men that grow bold, and wield a powerful weapon against this great evil; and even school boys daringly denounce a system, the enormity of which they cannot appreciate, surely I thought it may be permitted to one who has worn the galling yoke of bondage, to say something of its pains, and something of that freedom which, if he should not succeed in accurately defining, he can truly say he will ever admire and love.

JOHN THOMPSON.

Worcester, Mass., May, 1856.

Life of John Thompson, a Fugitive Slave.

CHAP. I.

I WAS born in Maryland, in 1812, and was slave to a Mrs. Wagar. She had four sons and two daughters. The sons were all farmers, owning large tracts of land; which were well stocked with slaves, and other animal property!

which he and his mother lived, and on which I was born. On this plantation were about two hundred slaves, young and old; of which fifty belonged to him, and the remainder to his mother; but all were in his charge.

Mr. J. H. W. had two children, John and Elizabeth. His wife died before I could remember, leaving the children under the supervision of the Grandmother. Elizabeth was about thirteen, and John ten years of age.

My parents had seven children, five sons and two daughters. My father and mother were field hands. My younger sister was house girl and ladies' maid, while the elder was given to one of the sons. The rest of us were too small to work, the eldest being only eleven years old.

The first act of slavery which I recorded in my mem-

2

ory, was the sale of my elder sister, who belonged to Henry Wagar, brother to J. H., and who lived three miles from our plantation. My mother heard of the sale, which was on Saturday, and on Sunday took us with her to see our beloved sister, who was then in the yard with the trader's drove, preparatory to being removed far south, on the Monday following. After travelling six miles, we arrived at our place of destination. Mother, approaching the door of the trader's house, fell upon her knees, in tears begging to be permitted to see her imprisoned daughter, who was soon to be dragged away from her embrace, probably to be seen no more in the flesh. It was not his custom to admit slaves into his yard to see

moved with compassion, for he opened the door, telling

Here, the first thing that saluted my ears, was the rattling of the chains upon the limbs of the poor victims. It seemed to me to be a hell upon earth, emblematical of that dreadful dungeon where the wicked are kept, until the day of God's retribution, and where their torment ascends up forever and ever.

As soon as my sister saw our mother, she ran to her and fell upon her neck, but was unable to speak a word. There was a scene which angels witnessed; there were tears which, I believe, were bottled and placed in God's depository, there to be reserved until the day when He shall pour His wrath upon this guilty nation.

The trader, becoming uneasy at this exciting scene, and fearing the rest of the drove would become dissatisfied with their situations, permitted sister to leave the yard for a few moments, to keep mother's company. He did not watch her, as I thought he would have done, but permitted her to go about with mother, and even to accompany us part of our way towards home. He ordered dinner for us, but not one of us could eat one mouthful. I thought my heart would break, as the time drew near for our departure. I dreaded the time when I should bid farewell to my beloved sister, never more to see her face, never more to meet her in the paternal circle, never more to hear her fervent prayer to the throne of God.

I watched the sun, as it seemed to descend behind the western hills; but this did not stop its progress. The time soon arrived when we must go. When mother was about to bid farewell to my sister, and reached out her hand to grasp hers, she burst into a flood of tears, exclaiming aloud. "Lord, have mercy upon me!"

The trader, seeing such parental affection, as he stood by, hung down his head and wiped the tears from his eyes; and to relieve himself from a scene so affecting, he said, "Mary, you can go some way with your mother, and return soon."

Turning to mother, he said, "old woman, I will do the best I can for your daughter; I will sell her to a good master."

We then left the house. After going with us two miles, sister Mary, in obedience to orders and her promise, could go no farther, and she said, "Mother, I suppose I must go back."

Here another heart-rending scene took place. I well

remember her parting words, "Mother," she said, "don't grieve, for though we are separated in body, our separation is only for a season, and if we are faithful we shall meet again where partings are no more. Mother, will you try to meet me?"

We all promised to do so. We then parted, and have never heard directly from her since. She was, as we afterwards understood, taken to Alabama, and sold at public auction. But, if I am faithful, I shall see her again.

Hark and hear the captive pleading,
  Listen to her plaintive cry,
While in floods her tears are falling;
  Must I, in my bondage die?
When I dwelt in my own country,
  With my children by my side,
Cruel white men coming on me,
  Dragg'd me o'er the deep so wide.
Oft I think of my sweet children,
  And my dear companion too;
If on earth I no more see them,
  And have bid a last adieu,
I must try to live so faithful
  To that God who rules above,
That I may obtain His favor,
  And may dwell with Him in love.
I must wait until that moment,
  When the trump of God shall sound;
Calling nations all together,
  Then to hear their final doom!
There I'll see my dear companion,
  Whom long since I bade adieu;
There I'll see my smiling children,
  And my blessed Jesus, too!
Then let cares, like a wild deluge,
  Roll across this mortal frame;
Death will soon burst off my fetters,
  Soon 'twill break the tyrant's chain;

Then I'll pass from grace to glory,
Then I'll sing my suffering o'er;
For then grief, and pain, and sorrow,
Shall be felt and known no more.

CHAP. II.

ALL the slaves, both men and women, except those about the house, were forced to work in the field. We raised corn, wheat and tobacco.

The provision for each slave, per week, was a peck of corn, two dozens of herrings, and about four pounds of meat. The children, under eight years of age, were not allowed anything. The women were allowed four weeks of leisure at child birth; after which, they were compelled to leave their infants to provide for themselves, and to the mercy of Providence, while they were again forced to labor in the field, sometimes a mile from the house.

Often the older children had to take care of the younger, sometimes the mother, until her babe was about three or four months old, if she had a kind and humane overseer, could come to the house once between meals, and nurse her child; but such favors were but seldom granted. More frequently the mother must take her child with her to the field, place it at the side where she could see it as she came to the end of the row; moving it along as she moved from row to row.

The slaves were called out from their quarters at daylight. The breakfast must be prepared and eaten before

2

going to work, and if not done before the overseer called
them to the field, they must go without it; and often the
children, being asleep at this time, were of course obliged
to go without their breakfast.

The slaves' clothing was, in winter, one shirt, pants
and jacket, without lining, shoes and stockings.   In sum-
mer, one shirt and one pair of pants of coarse linen.

When the tobacco is ripe, or nearly so, there are frequently worms in it, about two inches long, and as large
as one's thumb.   They have horns, and are called tobacco worms.   They are very destructive to the tobacco
crops, and must be carefully picked off by the hands, so
as not to break the leaves, which are very easily broken.
But careful as the slaves may be, they cannot well avoid
leaving some of these worms on the plants.   It was a
custom of Mr. Wagar to follow after the slaves, to see if
he could find any left, and if so, to compel the person in
whose row they were found, to eat them.   This was done
to render them more careful.   It may seem incredible to
my readers, but it is a fact.

My mistress and her family were all Episcopalians.
The nearest church was five miles from our plantation,
and there was no Methodist church nearer than ten miles.
So we went to the Episcopal church, but always came
home as we went, for the preaching was above our com-
prehension, so that we could understand but little that
was said.   But soon the Methodist religion was brought
among us, and preached in a manner so plain that the
way-faring man, though a fool, could not err therein.

This new doctrine produced great consternation among

the slaveholders. It was something which they could not understand. It brought glad tidings to the poor bondman ; it bound up the broken-hearted ; it opened the prison doors to them that were bound, and let the captive go free.

As soon as it got among the slaves, it spread from plantation to plantation, until it reached ours, where there were but few who did not experience religion. The slaveholders, becoming much alarmed at this strange phenomenon, called a meeting, at which they appointed men to patrol the country, and break up these religious assemblies. This was done, and many a poor victim had his back severely cut, for simply going to a prayer meeting.

At length, Mr. Wagar bought at auction a man named Martin, who was a fiddler. As slaves are very fond of dancing, our master thought that fiddling would bring them back to their former ignorant condition, and bought this man for that purpose. It had the desired effect upon most of them, and what the whip failed to accomplish, the fiddle completed, for it is no easy matter to drive a soul from God by cruelty, when it may easily be drawn away by worldly pleasures ; and fiddling I think is better appropriated to this purpose, than anything else I could mention.

CHAP. III.

MR. W. was a very cruel slave driver. He would whip unreasonably and without cause. He was often from home, and not unfrequently three or four weeks at a time, leaving the plantation, at such times, in care of the overseer. When he returned, he sometimes ordered all the slaves to assemble at the house, when he would whip them all round ; a little whipping being, as he thought, necessary, in order to secure the humble submission of the slaves.

Sometimes he forced one slave to flog another, the husband his wife ; the mother her daughter ; or the father his son. This practice seemed very amusing to himself and his children, especially to his son, John, who failed not to walk in his father's footsteps, by carrying into effeet the same principle, until he became characteristically a tyrant.

When at home ⁻from school, he would frequently request his grandmother's permission, to call all the black children from their quarters to the house, to sweep and clear the yard from weeds, &c., in order that he might oversee them. Then, whip in hand, he walked about among them, and sometimes lashed the poor little creatures, who had on nothing but a shirt, and often nothing at all, until the blood streamed down their backs and limbs, apparently for no reason whatever, except to gratify his own cruel fancy.

This was pleasing to his father and grandmother, who, accordingly, considered him a very smart boy indeed! Often, my mother, after being in the field all day, upon returning at night, would find her little children's backs mangled by the lash of John Wagar, or his grandmother ; for if any child dared to resist the boy, she would order the cook to lash it with a cowhide, kept for that purpose.

I well remember the tears of my poor mother, as they fell upon my back, while she was bathing and dressing my wounds. But there was no redress for her grievance, she had no appeal for justice, save to high heaven; for if she complained, her own back would be cut in a similar manner.

Sometimes she wept and sobbed all night, but her tears must be dried and her sobs hushed, ere the overseer's horn sounded, which it did at early dawn, lest they should betray her. And she, unrefreshed, must shake off her dull slumbers, and repair, at break of day, to the field, leaving her little ones to a similar, or perhaps, worse fate on the coming day, and dreading a renewal of her own sorrows the coming evening. Great God, what a succession of crimes! Is there no balm in Gilead; is there no physician there, that thy people can be healed?

Martin, the fiddler, was bought for a term of ten years, after which he was to be freed. He was a good hand, was called a faithful, humble servant, and was much liked by all who knew him. His term was now expired, according to the bill of sale. Of this he was fully sensible, but his administrator being at the distance of seventy-five miles from him, Martin had no means of seeing him, nor of informing him that he was still held in bondage, beyond the time of contract.

Therefore, feeling himself at liberty, he consequently began to manifest some signs of his freedom; for, when the overseer would drive him as usual, he wanted him to understand that what he now did was optional with himself, since he was now a free man, and had been such for eighteen months.

The overseer took this as an insult, but would not correct him himself, for he feared the action of Martin's administrator. Accordingly he complained to Mr. W., upon his return from a journey, upon which he had been absent. Martin was immediately called up, together with all the slaves, that they might witness the punishment to which he was subjected, in order that it might prove a warning to any one who might fancy himself free.

None knew at the time why they were called; they only knew that some one, and perhaps all, were to be whipped. And immediately each one began to inquire within himself, is it I? They began to consider if they had done anything worthy of punishment. Their doubts and fears were, however, soon ended by the lot falling on Martin, who was ordered to cross his hands. This was in the barn yard. He, having had his coarse shirt removed, and his pants fastened about his hips, was swung up to a beam by his hands, in the open shed, when the overseer was ordered to lash him with a cowhide. Every stroke laid open the flesh upon his back, and caused the blood to flow. His shrieks and piteous cries of "Lord, have mercy on me!" were heard at distant plantations. But they were of no avail; there was no mercy in the iron heart of his tormentor. It seemed as if death alone could terminate his sufferings. But at length God heard his cry, and sent deliverance. By a weak and unexpected means, He confounded the mighty.

John, who at this time was about fifteen years of age,

was out gunning, at a distance from the house. He heard the piercing shrieks of the victim, and hastened to the spot, where the frightful scene was being enacted.

"What is the overseer whipping Martin for," he inquired of his father.

His father answered the question only by bidding him go to the house. Instead of obeying, John cocked his gun, exclaiming "by God, I'll kill that overseer!" at the same time pointing the weapon at the overseer, and bidding his father to stand out of his way.

The overseer, becoming frightened, ran to Mr. Wagar for safety, well knowing that John would execute his threat, and that separated from Mr. W. there was no safety for him.

"Put up that gun, John," said his father.

"No I won't," replied John, "stand away, stand away, I'll kill that d—d overseer!"

The father was afraid to go towards his own son, lest in the frenzy of exasperation, he should murder him. So the overseer, conducted by Mr. W., for safety, left the farm for two days, until John's anger was appeased. Martin was then cut down by John, but was not able to work for several days.

About four or five months after this occurrence, his administrator arrived at the plantation. He seemed much surprised·that Martin had been held so long over his time, and said that Mr. W. should pay him for it. He said nothing of the unjust punishment Martin had received, and whether there was ever any redress for it, I never knew. Martin left this plantation for a better one.

This was the only good act of John Wagar, of which I ever knew. Ever afterwards he was fully equal to his father in cruelty. Not many years afterwards, he whipped a slave woman to death, for taking a glass of rum out of his jug, which he thought he had lost.

This woman's husband generally kept liquor in his house, where some was found, when search was made in the slave's quarters for the lost rum. She said that her husband had bought it, but her assertion was not credited. Her husband belonged to a Mr. Morton, about five miles distant, and came on Saturdays to see his wife. The woman's name was Minta; she was the mother of six children. She was whipped to make her confess she was guilty, when she was not; and she finally confessed. He whipped her one half hour, to force a confession; after which he whipped another half hour for a crime which she never committed. This caused her death, which occurred three days after.

This was about the commencement of John's administration, for after he had finished his education and returned home, his father gave up the management of the plantation to him.

While young and attending school, his uncle gave him a beautiful little pony, saddle and bridle. Then this young gentleman must have a private body servant for himself, and he claimed the honor of making choice of one for himself, from among the slave children. Accordingly he made choice of myself.

Then my business was to wait upon him, attend to his horse, and go with him to and from school; for neglect of which, as he fancied, I often got severe floggings from him. Still, I did not wish my situation changed, for I considered my station a very high one; preferring an occasional licking, to being thrown out of office.

Being a gentleman's body servant, I had nothing more to do with plantation affairs, and, consequently, thought myself much superior to those children who had to sweep the yard. I was about twelve years old when given to John Wagar.

CHAP. IV.

FIDDLING and dancing being done away with among the slaves, by the disappearance of Martin's fiddle, Christianity seemed to gain ground, and a glorious revival of religion sprang up, which required another legal provision to suppress. This was the new provision: that the patrolers should search the slave quarters, on every plantation, from whence, if they found any slaves absent after night fall, they should receive, when found, thirty-nine lashes upon the naked back. When the slaves were caught, if a constable were present, he could administer the punishment immediately. If no constable were present, then the truant slave must be taken before a justice of the peace, where he must receive not less than five, nor more than thirty-nine lashes, unless he could show a pass, either from his master or his overseer. Many were thus whipped, both going to and returning from night meetings; or, worse still, often taken from their knees while at prayer, and cruelly whipped.

But this did not stop the progress of God's mighty work, for he had laid the foundation for the building, and his workmen determined to carry on the work until the capstone was laid.

Many slaves were sold farther south, for going to meetings. They would sometimes travel four or five miles, attend meeting and return in time for the overseer's horn.

Mr. Wagar had a valuable slave named Aaron, a carpenter by trade, and an excellent workman; a man of true piety and great physical strength. He never submitted to be flogged, unless compelled by superior force; and although he was often whipped, still it did not conquer his will, nor lessen his bravery; so that, whenever his master attempted to whip him, it was never without the assistance of, at least, five or six men. Such men there were who were always ready to lend their aid in such emergencies. Aaron was too valuable to shoot, and his master did not wish to sell him; but at last, growing tired of calling on help to whip a slave, and knowing that neglecting to do this would appear like a submission to the negro, which in time might prove dangerous, since other slaves, becoming unruly, might resist him, until he could not flog any of them without help. He finally concluded to sell Aaron, much as he disliked it.

The slave was at work at the time, sawing heavy timber, to build a barn. The manner of sawing such timber, at the South, is by what they call a whip saw. A scaffold, about ten feet high, being erected, the logs to be sawed are placed thereon, when one man is placed above, and another below, who alternately pull and push the saw, thus forcing it through the logs.

Aaron was busy at this kind of work, when he observed several strange visitors approaching him, whose business he did not at first suspect. He was requested to come down from the scaffold, as one of the gentlemen wished to talk with him about building a barn. He at once refused to comply with the request, for having seen the same trader before, he soon surmised his business, and supposed that he, himself, was sold.

At this refusal, they commenced pelting him with stones, chips, or whatever else they could find to throw at him, until they finally forced him down. He sprang from the scaffold, axe in hand, and commenced trying to cut his way through them ; but, being defeated, he was knocked down, put in irons, taken to the drove yard, and beaten severely, but not until he had badly wounded two of his captors.

His wife, being at the house spinning wool, did not hear of this until night. In the anguish of her heart, she ran, weeping bitterly, from one plantation to another, in search of some kind slaveholder who would buy her husband. But, alas, she could find none.

Aaron was kept confined in the jail yard two weeks, during every day of which he was whipped. Finally he broke jail and made his escape. The trader came early next morning to his jail, but Aaron was not there. At that time the slaves knew little of the friendly guidance of the north star, and therefore lingered about in swamps and among bushes, where they were fed by their fellow servants during the night, instead of fleeing to the north.

In this way Aaron remained concealed nearly one year, after which his wife got a man to purchase him, a running. Then Uncle Aaron came home to his new master, where he was when I left the South.

Matters continued in about the same course until the year 1822, when a change took place on our plantation, caused by the death of old Mistress, which event happened in October of that year. Now her slaves must be divided among her children and grand children. Now we must pass into other hands, some for better, some for worse.

The estate was divided the same month in which old Mistress died. The slaves were also divided, and each one was to go to his new home on the first of January, 1823. My father's family fell to Mr. George Thomas, who was a cruel man, and all the slaves feared much that they should fall to him. He was a very bad man. He fed his slaves well, but drove and whipped them most unmercifully, and not unfrequently selling them.

The time drew near for our departure, and sorrowful it was. Every heart was sad ; every countenance downcast. Parents looking upon their darling children would say, " is it possible that I must soon bid them adieu, possibly forever !" Some rejoiced in hope of a better situation, while others mourned, fearing a worse one. Christmas came, but without bringing the usual gladness and joy. We met together in prayer meeting, and petitioned for heavenly strength to sustain our feeble frames. These were continued during holiday week, from Christmas to New Year's day, when slaves are not to be molested; consequently, no patrolers annoyed us.

New Year's, that sorrowful day for us, at length arrived. Each one weeping while they went round, taking leave of parents or children, for some children and parents were separated, as were also husbands and wives. Our meetings were now broken up, and our separation accomplished.

CHAP. V.

I WAS about fourteen years of age when the change mentioned in the last chapter, occurred. John Wagar claimed me by promise, as he said my grandmother gave me to him; and, consequently, bade me keep out of sight, when they came for my father's family. This I did by hiding myself until the rest were all gone. I did this willingly, as I did not want to go to Mr. Thomas. Indeed, I had rather forego the pleasure of being with my parents than live with him. So I remained behind.

I had lived securely upon the old plantation about three months, when one day I was sent on an errand, two or three miles from home. There I met Mr. Thomas, who said to me, "where are you going?" I answered his question, when he said, "You belong to me; come, go home

3

with me." I told him I wished to return with my errand, but he said "No; go right home to my house, where your father and mother are. Don't you want to see your mother?" I replied that I did, for I was afraid to answer any other way.

This Mr. George Thomas had married my old Mistress's daughter, and we fell to him in right of his wife. I went home with him with a heavy heart.

When John Wagar heard of this event, he said I belonged to him and should come back; but he could not accomplish his purpose in this, for being left to Mrs. Thomas, he could not hold me. He then tried to buy me, but my new master would not sell me, to him.

Soon after my arrival in the family, Mr. Thomas let me to one of his sons, named Henry, who was a doctor, to attend his horse. This son was unmarried, lived a bachelor, and kept a cook and waiter. The cook belonged neither to him nor his father, but was hired. She was a good looking mulatto, and was married to a right smart, intelligent man, who belonged to the doctor's uncle. One night, coming home in haste, and wishing to see his wife, he sent me up stairs to request her to come down. Upon going up, I found she was in a room with the doctor, the door of which was fast. This I thoughtlessly told her husband, who, upon her coming down a moment after, upbraided her for it. She denied it, and afterwards told the doctor, but not till I had gone to my mother, sick, up to the old man's plantation.

The doctor was a very intemperate man. As soon as his cook told him her story, he came to his father with the complaint, that I had left him without his consent; upon which his father told him to flog me. He ordered me out to the barn, when I was scarcely able to hold up my head, and had to be led by my brother.

Without saying what he wanted of me, he stripped off my clothes and then whipped me, beating me over the head until I became senseless, and life was nearly extinct. I was carried to my mother's quarters, where I lay five weeks, unable to move without assistance. When I finally recovered, I did not return to him, as he did not wish it, but remained with my mother four years.

My father was a very pious man, never complaining, but bearing every thing patiently, and praying for grace and fortitude to help him to overcome his trials, which he believed would one day be ended. He was a good servant and an affectionate parent. But new trials and sorrows soon broke upon this quiet family.

My sister, whose name I must not mention, as she is now in the North, and like myself, not out of danger, was old Mistress's house maid. She possessed both grace and beauty, and to-day, thank God, is a living monument in his temple. She was given to Mrs. Thomas as her maid, and was much prized, because a gift from her mother; but especially because she knew her to be a virtuous girl.

She had found it impossible to long keep a maid of this stamp, for none could escape the licentious passions of her husband, who was the father of about one-fourth of the slaves on his plantation, by his slave women. Mrs. Thomas strove every way to shield my sister from this monster, but he was determined to accomplish his brutal designs.

One day during his wife's absence on a visit to her friends, being, as he thought, a good opportunity, he tried to force my sister to submit to his wishes. This she defeated by a resistance so obstinate, that he, becoming enraged, ordered two of his men to take her to the barn, where he generally whipped his slaves; there to strip off her clothes and whip her, which was done, until the blood stood in puddles under her feet.

Upon his wife's return, Mr. Thomas told her that my sister had been whipped for neglect of duty. Of this Mrs. Thomas did not complain, as she had no objection to necessary floggings. But similar scenes occuring quite often, our Mistress began to suspect that sister was not in fault, especially as in her presence she never neglected her business, and these complaints only came during her absence. Besides, she knew well her husband's former practices, and at last began to suspect that these and my sister's pretended faults, were in some way connected. Accordingly, she began to question her maid concerning her offences, who, fearing to tell her plainly, knowing it would be certain death to her, answered in low and trembling terms, " I must not tell you, but you may know what it is all for. If I have done anything, Madam, contrary to your wishes, and do not suit you, please sell me, but do not kill me without cause. Old Mistress, your mother, who is dead, and I trust in heaven, took great pains to bring me up a virtuous girl, and I will die before I will depart from her dying counsel, given, as you well know, while we were standing by her dying bed."

These words so affected Mrs. Thomas, that she fainted and was carried to her bed, to which she was confined by sickness five or six weeks. Her husband's conduct still persisted in, finally caused her death, which occurred four years after.

Mistress told sister that she had best get married, and that if she would, she would give her a wedding. Soon after, a very respectable young man, belonging to Mr. Bowman, a wealthy planter, and reputed to be a good master, began to court my sister. This very much pleased Mistress, who wished to hasten the marriage. She determined that her maid should be married, not as slaves usually are, but that with the usual matrimonial ceremonies should be tied the knot to be broken only by death.

The Sabbath was appointed for the marriage, which was to take place at the Episcopal Church. I must here state that no slave can be married lawfully, without a line from his or her owner. Mistress and all the family, except the old man, went to church to witness the marriage ceremony, which was to be performed by their minister, parson Reynolds. The master of Josiah, my sister's destined husband, was also at the wedding, for he thought a great deal of his man.

Mistress returned delighted from the wedding, for she thought she had accomplished a great piece of work. But the whole affair only enraged her unfeeling husband, who, to be revenged upon the maid, proposed to sell her. To this his wife refused consent. Although Mrs. T. had never told him her suspicions, or what my sister had said, yet he suspected the truth, and determined to be revenged. Accordingly, during another absence of Mistress, he again cruelly whipped my sister. A continued repetition of these things finally killed our Mistress, who the doctor said, died of a broken heart.

After the death of this friend, sister ran away, leaving behind her husband and one child, and finally found her way to the North. None of our family ever heard from her afterwards, until I accidentally met her in the streets in Philadelphia. My readers can imagine what a meeting ours must have been. She is again married and in prosperity.

CHAP. VI.

My master, George Thomas, was a man of wealth, his farm consisting of about one thousand acres of land, well stocked with slaves. He was as inhuman as he was rich, and would whip when no particle of fault existed on the part of the slave. He would not employ an overseer who did not practice whipping one or more slaves at least once a day; if not a man, then some weak or gray-headed woman. Any overseer who would not agree to these terms, could find no employment on Mr. Thomas's farm.

The third year after our arrival upon his plantation, he hired an overseer from Virginia, who was a man after his own heart, and who commenced the work of bloodshed soon after his arrival. He, however, soon met with his match.

On the plantation was a slave named Ben, who was highly prized by Mr. T., being, as he thought, the best and most faithful servant on the farm. Ben was a resolute and brave man, and did not fear death. Such courage did not suit the overseer, who wanted each slave to temble with fear when he addressed him. .Ben was too high-minded for such humiliation before any insignificant overseer. He had philosophically concluded that death is but death any way, and that one might as well die by hanging as whipping ; so he resolved not to submit to be whipped by the overseer.

One day in the month of November, when the slaves were in the field gathering corn, which Ben was carting to the barn, the overseer thought he did not drive his oxen fast enough. As soon then as Ben came within hearing of his voice, while returning from the barn, where he had just discharged his load, to the field, the overseer bellowed to him to drive faster. With this order Ben attempted to comply, by urging his beasts to their utmost speed. But all was of no avail. As soon as they met, the overseer struck Ben upon the head with the butt of his whip, felling him to the ground. But before he could repeat the blow, Ben sprang. from the ground, seized his antagonist by the throat with one hand, while he felled him to the ground with the other ; then jumping upon his breast, he commenced choking and beating him at the same time, until he had nearly killed him. In fact he probably would have killed his enemy, had not two of

the slaves hastened to his rescue, which they with difficulty accomplished, so firm and determined was Ben's
hold of him.   For a while the discomfited man was senseless, his face became of the blackness of his hat, while
the blood streamed down his face.

When he had recovered his senses, and was able to
walk, he started for the house, to relate this sad circumstance to Mr. Thomas.   Ben loaded his cart and followed
after.   No sooner had he entered the barn, than his master sprang forward to seize him; but Ben eluded his
grasp and fled to the woods, where he remained about
three weeks, when he returned to his work.

No allusion was made to the circumstance for about
five weeks, and Ben supposed all was past and forgotten.   At length a rainy time came on, during which the
hands could neither labor in the field nor elsewhere out
of doors, but were forced to work in the corn-house, shell-
ing the corn.   While all were thus busily employed, the
doors closed, there entered five strong white men, besides
our master, armed with pistols, swords, and clubs.   What
a shocking sight! thus to take one poor unarmed negro,
these men must be employed, and the county aroused to
action.

Ben was soon bound in hemp enough, comparatively
speaking, to rig a small vessel.   Thus bound, he was led
to the place of torture, where he was whipped until his
entrails could be seen moving within his body.   Poor
Ben! his crime, according to the laws of Maryland, was
punishable with death; a penalty far more merciful than
the one he received.

The manner of whipping on Mr. Thomas's plantation, was to bind the victim fast, hands, body and feet, around a hogshead or cask, so that he was unable to move. After Ben was thus flogged, he said, "I wish I had killed the overseer, then I should have been hung. and an end put to my pain. If I have to do the like again, I will kill him and be hung at once!"

Ben was, for five weeks, unable to walk, or sit, or lie down. He could only rest upon his knees and elbows, and his wounds became so offensive, that no person could long remain in his presence. He crawled about upon his hands and knees, gritting his teeth with pain and vengeance, and often exclaiming, "How I wish I had taken his life!"

After this, Mr. Thomas forbade his overseers meddling with Ben, telling them that he would kill them if they did ; also, that he was a good hand, and needed no driving. When Ben got well, Mr. Thomas knowing his disposition, was afraid to go near or speak to him ; consequently, he was sent to a distant part of the farm to work by himself, nor was he ever again struck by master or overseer.

Ben was a brave fellow, nor did this flogging lessen his bravery in the least. Nor is Ben the only brave slave at the South ; there are many there who would rather be shot than whipped by any man.

After I had learned to read, I was very fond of reading newspapers, when I could get them. One day in the year 1830, I picked up a piece of old newspaper containing the speech of J. Q. Adams, in the U. S. Senate, upon

4

a petition of the ladies of Massachusetts, praying for the abolition of slavery in the District of Columbia. This I kept hid away for some months, and read it until it was so worn that I could scarce make out the letters.

While reading this speech, my heart leaped with joy. I spent many Sabbaths alone in the woods, meditating upon it. I then found out that there was a place where the negro was regarded as a man, and not as a brute; where he might enjoy the "inalienable right of life, liberty, and the pursuit of happiness"; and where he could walk unfettered throughout the length and breadth of the land.

These thoughts were constantly revolving in my mind, and I determined to see, ere long, the land from whence echoed that noble voice ; where man acknowledged a difference between his brother man and a beast ; and where I could "worship God under my own vine and fig tree, with none to molest or make afraid."

Little did Mr. Adams know, when he was uttering that speech, that he was "opening the eyes of the blind"; that he was breaking the iron bands from the limbs of one poor slave, and setting the captive free. But bread cast upon the waters, will be found and gathered after many days.

But Mr. Adams has gone from hope to reward, and while his mortal body is laying in the dust of the earth, awaiting the summons for the re-union of soul and body, his spirit is with God in his kingdom above.

CHAP. VII.

NEAR our plantation lived as cruel a planter as ever God suffered to live, named doctor Jackson; who was the owner of a large farm, with several slaves. He was destitute of heart, soul, and conscience; while his wife was of the same character. She often induced him to illtreat the slaves, especially those about the house; she being as ready to complain of them, as he was to punish them.

One day, she became displeased with Sarah, her cook, and wanted her husband to whip her. She said to Sarah, " I swear I will make your master whip you, as soon as he comes to the house "; to which Sarah replied, " Those who will swear, will lie !" This reply she reported to the doctor upon his return; upon which he tied Sarah up and whipped her, until the flesh so cleaved from the bone, that it might easily have been scraped off with the hand; while the blood stood in puddles under her feet.

After taking her down, he anointed her lacerated back with a mixture of grease and tar, which was a new application; the usual one being strong brine. For a long time after this, the poor creature could neither walk nor stand, and it was dreadful to see her crawling about in such painful agony. To Mrs. Jackson, however, it was a delightful sight, for she seemed to gloat over the sight of such bloody, mangled victims. Her cook had often before been flogged, but never so much to her satisfaction.

I was one day sent upon an errand to the doctor's

house, and being acquainted, I did not ask permission to enter, but went in unannounced at the dining-room door. There I saw a little slave girl, about eight years of age, running about the room ; while Mrs. Jackson was following and lashing her, and the blood running upon the floor ! The child's offense was breaking a dish !!

On another side of our plantation lived another tyrant, by name Clinton Hanley ; who also had a large farm well stocked with slaves. In his cruelty, this man had invented a somewhat different way of punishing his slaves, from that practised by most masters. He whipped severely, drove hard, and fed poorly. In cold weather he sent his slaves, both men and women, through the snow, without shoes, to cut wood.

He had one slave, named Mary, who was thus sent out to cut wood, until her feet were so frozen and cracked, that she could be tracked by her blood. To punish her, he one day ordered two men to lift up the fence and put her head under, while he sat upon it to increase the weight. While thus occupied, he was suddenly seized with a violent pain at his heart, of which he died within three days.

I was hired out one year to a Mr. Compton, who was a kind master ; feeding and clothing well, and seldom beating his slaves, of which he owned about one hundred able bodied and intelligent men and women. His wife was equally as kind as a Mistress.

Mr. Compton was a sportsman, and very fond of gaming, horse racing and drinking. His slaves were all religious, and much attached to their master and mistress.

They were allowed to hold their prayer meetings unmolested, in their own quarters, and I felt thankful that I had once more got among Christians.

Mr. Compton finally got so in debt, by his extravagance, that he was obliged to sell his slaves to pay his creditors. The slaves, little suspecting for what purpose, were sent down to town to pack tobacco. While busily engaged at this work, the warehouse door was suddenly closed, to prevent their escaping; when about sixty of them were fettered and put on board a schooner, then lying at anchor in the river, for the express purpose of conveying them far to the South. Only three were fortunate enough to make their escape. The women and children were brought down from the farm in wagons, and put on board the vessel.

But O! reader, could you have seen those men, loaded down with irons, as they passed weeping from the warehouse, you must have exclaimed, "Great God, how long wilt thou suffer this sin to remain upon the earth?"

The three men who made their escape, were sold to new masters.

Mrs. Compton, being from home at the time, knew nothing of this transaction until her return. When she first heard of it, she fainted; but upon recovering exclaimed, in the anguish of her heart, "O, my people; husband, my heart will break!"

But her tears were of no avail; it was too late; the vessel, freighted with its human cargo, had already weighed anchor, and was under sail. Wafted by the northern breeze she gallantly sailed down the stream at the rate of

nine knots per hour ; while the multitude stood upon the
banks and watched her disappearance, tears of pity flow-
ing down their cheeks.

She soon vanished from their sight. But God, who
has his ways in the wind, and manages the sea, had his
purpose fixed ; so thought one of the slaves, who, in his
faith, raised his cry of petition to the living God ; so
while some were dancing to please the captain and crew,
others were crying.

The vessel ran well for about four days, when suddenly the sky became overcast with dense black clouds, from
whence flashed the forked lightnings, and pealed the fearful thunders. The raging billows lashed into fury, rolled
mountain high, until there seemed no possible escape from
the frowns of a sin-avenging God. The captain summoned
all hands on board, and the vessel was finally driven upon a sand beach, near one of the West India Islands,
where all on board, except one of the sailors, was saved.
And thus did these slaves obtain their freedom. The
trader himself was not on board, having gone by land, to
the place where he expected to meet the slaves, after
giving them in charge to another person.

From this time to the day of her death, Mrs. Compton always wore the marks of a sorrowful woman, while
her husband became a miserable wretch. In consequence
of his inability to pay my year's wages, I only remained
with him until Christmas ; after which I was hired out
to Richard Thomas, my mistress's brother ; who was the
most humane of the family, and who, notwithstanding he
liked to whip them himself, did not choose that any one

else should chastise his slaves. I lived with him two years.

He had a hired plantation about thirty-five miles from his father's, where were my father, mother and five brothers; all having been hired out to him. Here I had an opportunity of improving in my education, for many of the planters in this region were not only rich, but humane, and many of their slaves could read and write. Miserable loafing white people were scarce in that vicinity, their services not being needed. Neither was slave hunting much practised, therefore there was no patroling, and the land being less cursed by cruelty, was rich and fertile; producing in abundance corn, wheat, and tobacco, together with cotton enough for home consumption.

Religion also flourished in that region, where there were no Catholic churches, but only Methodists and Episcopalians. Finally the masters concluded to build a church for their slaves. So they united in the work and soon had a large church, under the superintendance of a white preacher; although a colored man could preach in it, if qualified and licensed by the whites. The congregation was large. Many white people went there to hear the colored ones sing and praise God, and were often much affected by their simple but earnest devotion.

Mr. Thomas, being a lawyer of great reputation and extensive practise, was necessarily often called from home on business, disconnected with his farm; consequently he employed an overseer to attend to this and the slaves. This overseer was a very proud and haughty fellow, made so by this sudden promotion; he never before having held such an office, which made him fancy himself, if not a god, at least an emperor!

Our living, which before had been decent, he soon entirely changed; frequently allowing us but one meal of victuals a day, consisting of corn bread, sometimes baked in the ashes, with two salted herring. This was to be eaten before going to the field in the morning, and we were called at break of day, after which we had no more until our return at night. Now you must know, reader, that chopping wood all day, upon an empty stomach, is not what it is cracked up to be!

One cold winter's day in February he sent us to the woods to chop. I worked until I became so hungry and faint, that I thought I could stand it no longer, when I resolved to go to the house for something to eat; or failing, to die in the attempt. Some of the hands promising to follow me, I started, supposing them close at hand; but I soon found myself alone, they having backed out, their courage failing. They thought, as I had troubled the waters, I might drink them alone; but they declined to partake of such bitter streams.

Before I reached the house, the overseer saw me and inquired where I was bound, to which I replied, "to the house, for something to eat." He ordered me back, but I, being homeward bound, and under full sail, thought best not to 'bout ship, so he ran after me, caught me by the back of the neck, struck me with the butt end of the whip upon my head, but did not fell me to the ground. I seized hold of the whip, wrung it from his hand, threw him upon the ground, clenched him somewhere about the throat, and for a few moments stopped his mortal respiration.

When I released him, he lost no time in running for the house, to tell his story to master Richard; after which he hastened back to the woods. I went to our quarters, ate my corn cake and herrings, and returned to the chopping. Nothing was said; the silence of the grave seemed to reign around, broken only by the sound of the axes. The men seemed to cut more wood that afternoon, than at other times they had for a whole day.

Next morning upon going, as usual, to the stable to attend to the horses, the overseer followed me, entered the stable and shut the door. He took from his pocket a rope, and ordered me to cross my hands, which I refused to do; upon which he seized a tobacco stick about four feet long and two inches thick, with which he struck and brought me to the ground. He then sprang upon me, for the purpose of tying my hands, but did not succeed, for I rose to my feet with him upon my back, shook off my uncomfortable load, and in turn mounted his back, wrung the stick from his hand, and with it commenced beating him.

As soon as he could escape from my hands, he opened the stable door and ran for the house; from whence I soon saw him returning in great haste, accompanied by master Richard; who, coming up to me, bade me surrender. I did so, and he tied my hands across each other, then tied me to one of the beams in the barn, and told the overseer to whip me. Accordingly he divested himself of his coat, rolled up his sleeves, and commenced

flogging with all his might.   But after giving me about
ten cuts, to his extreme disappointment, he was told to
desist, as that was sufficient.

I thought much of being thus punished for nothing,
and resolved that, should the overseer again attempt to
whip me, I would kill him and abide the consequences.
I therefore told master Richard, that I had rather die
than again be whipped ; that the punishment of death
was not so dreadful, and I should know next time what
to do. "What will you do, sir ?" said he.   I replied,
" You alone have the right to correct me, sir.   Had you
been made acquainted with all the facts in the case, you
would not have had me whipped so ; and if the overseer
strikes me again, I will kill him and be hung at once,
that there may be an end of me."   He bade me hold my
tongue, and go to work ; after which, turning to the
overseer, he said, " Whenever that fellow disobeys,
I wish you to inform me, that I may learn what is the
fault ; I do not wish you to flog him ; I know he is a
good hand, and needs no flogging to make him work."

After this, we had three meals a day, larger in proportion, and everything went on well, until the following
July, when a difficulty arose between master and overseer.

CHAP. VIII.

My young master, being very fond of work himself,
did not like to see lazy men around him.   Whenever he
came to the field, he always busied himself about some-

thing, while the overseer stood with his whip under his arm, and his hands in his pockets, or sat under a shady tree and read the newspapers. I well knew this would not last very long, and had the overseer known his employer as well as I did, he would not thus have hazarded his best interest by an indulgence in such laziness, as finally dethroned him.

Master Richard, coming into the field one day, found the overseer, as usual, sitting at his ease under a pleasant tree, which at once irritated him. Addressing the overseer, as he was thus enjoying his comfort, he asked, "Why have not the ploughs been used in this field, where they are so much needed, instead of yonder, where they are less needed?"

The overseer made some paltry reply, not so well suited to master's dignity, as to the purpose which he had in contemplation, which was to discharge him immediately; a thing which, according to contract, he could not do. Directly, upon hearing the answer, he seized a stick which lay near, and with it aimed a violent blow at the overseer's head, which, however, he fortunately dodged, when he ran from the field, left the plantation, and was seen there no more.

My father was then put overseer, an office which he did not long fill, as in October following he sickened and died. His death was much lamented by all his fellow slaves, as well as by his master, Richard, who gave him every possible attention during his sickness, employing the best physicians to attend upon him. He called to see him three or four times each day, and sometimes sat by his bedside hours at a time, apparently striving to prevent the extinction of the vital spark ; but all to no purpose, for the great Master had called for him, and he must obey the summons.

My father lived an exemplary life, and died a triumphant death, leaving to posterity a bright evidence of his acceptance with God.   And, thank heaven, his prayers over me, a careless, hardened sinner, were not as seed sown upon a rock, but as bread cast upon the waters, to be seen and gathered after many days.

Immediately after the decease of this faithful slave, master Richard directed my brother to take his horse and go up to old master's plantation, and inform his sister Elizabeth, our mistress, that his father, John, her slave, was dead.   As soon as she received the tidings, she came in her carriage to her brother's, but only to look on the lifeless clay of my father.   " Oh ! " she exclaimed, as she gazed upon the lifeless form, "I had rather lose all my other slaves, than to lose John."   ·

My brother was now put overseer, and made an excellent one.   The crops, in their abundance, were gathered and safely secured.

We now removed about forty miles to another plantation, in Prince George county, a neighborhood as different from that we had just left, as Alabama is from Kentucky. Here our master married a Miss Barber, very rich and equally cruel.   I think she was about as bad a woman as ever lived.   She soon spoiled her husband's disposition, inducing in him the practice of the surrounding planters, to whip occasionally, whether there was a cause or not. They considered whipping as essential to the good of the soul as the body; and therefore sometimes indispensably necessary.

My old grey-headed mother, now cook, was the first victim to the uncontrollable, hellish passions of her new mistress. My mother had always borne the reputation, in old mistress's time, of a very good cook; but she could not suit this tyrannical mistress, do the best she could. Indeed, nothing was so pleasant to her as the smell of negro blood! Entering the kitchen, she would beat my mother with shovel, tongs, or whatever other weapon lay within her reach, until exhausted herself; then, upon her husband's return, she would complain to him, and cause him to strip and whip the victim until she was unable longer to stand. My feelings, upon hearing her shrieks and pleadings, may better be imagined than described. Sometimes she would, in this way, have all her servants whipped.

While upon the other plantation, I spared no exertions to learn to read and write, both of which I could now do tolerably well; and although I spent all my Sundays in study, still, master did not know that I could do either. One day he sent me with a note to a gentleman, requiring an answer by the bearer. The answer I put into my pocket with some writing of my own, one of which was the copy of a pass I had received from my master long before, to go to visit a friend. This copy I accidentally handed him, instead of the answering note, not perceiving my mistake until he exclaimed, " What is this?" Immediately I discovered my mistake, and handed him the

5

right paper. He kept both. At the time he said no
more to me, but soon communicated the fact to his
sister, pressing her to sell me, which she at length
consented to do, empowering him to transact the business in reference to the sale. The next morning,
while I was preparing feed for the horses in the
stables, he, with four other white men, armed with
bludgeons and pistols, came upon me. I looked about
me for some means of resistance, but seeing none, concluded there was no way for me but to surrender.

My hands were at once tied, after which I was taken
to another part of the barn, where they commenced
whipping me ; but the switches proving brittle, two of
them were broken at once. This so enraged my master
that he cursed the switches, and swore he had something
that would not break. This was a cowhide, which he
went and brought from the house, I, meanwhile, hanging
suspended between the heavens and the earth, for no
crime save what he himself was guilty of, namely, education. He finally concluded, however, not to whip me,
lest it might injure my sale, and therefore ordered one of
the other slaves to take me down, and prepare me to go
to Alexandria.

All being ready, he called for me to be brought out.
As I passed the house door in crossing the yard, bound
in chains, his wife came out and ordered me to stop a
moment, while she delivered to me her farewell message.

" Well, John," she began, " you are going to be sold !"
" Yes, madam, I suppose so," was my reply.

" I am sorry," she continued, " that you are so disobedient to your master Richard, and if you will promise me to do better, I will plead with him not to sell you."

I answered, " Madam, I have done the best I am able for him, and cannot, to save my life, do better ; willingly would I do so, if I could. I do not know why he wishes to sell me."

While I was speaking, he came out, being ready to start for the slave market. He said to his wife, " I don't wish you to speak to him, for I am going to sell him ; sister Elizabeth gave me leave to do so, and I shall do it." " He has promised me to do better, and I do not wish him sold," said his wife.

" I don't want to hear any of his promises, he has made them before," was his reply.

While this conversation was going on, a coachman from the lower plantation rode up, and handed master Richard a note, saying that Miss Elizabeth had changed her mind, and did not wish me sold, and that if he did not want me any longer, to send me home to her. Thus was the affair knocked into a cocked hat.

He took the rope from my hands, and bade me go to work, a command which I joyfully obeyed ; but feeling no gratitude to him, since, had it been in his power, he would have sold me. I finished my year with him, after which, on Christmas, I returned to my mistress.

CHAP. IX.

THE following year, I was hired to Mr. Wm. Barber, a Catholic himself, as were also his slaves, all except myself. He adhered strictly to his religious profession, praying three or four times each day, and every Sunday morning calling up his slaves to attend prayer, to which call I refused to respond. This refusal in me, caused in him a strong dislike to me, insomuch that he seemed to dislike me, and hate to see me worse than the devil, against whom he prayed so devoutly.

I was very fond of singing Methodist hymns while at work, especially if I was alone, the sound of which threw him into spasms of anger. He accordingly treated me worse than any other slave upon the plantation, all of whom were treated bad enough. Our allowance was a quart of meal and two herrings per day. Our dinner was sent to us in the fields, both in hot and cold weather. None of our friends were ever permitted to come to the farm to see us.

On Easter, it being holiday among the slaves, a negro belonging to Mr. Charles Gardner, not knowing our master's rules, called to see his mother and sister, whom Mr. Barber had hired, and whom he had not seen for a long time. Our master happening to get a glimpse of this negro, pitched upon him and endeavored to collar him. The black, being a strong active fellow, and understanding what we call the "Virginia hoist," seized and threw his assailant over his head to the distance of five feet, where he struck the ground so that his nose ploughed the earth some distance ! Before the discomfited master could rise from the ground, the slave had effected his escape.

But poor David's back must smart for his dexterity. Master imagined that I invited David to our plantation for the purpose of retaliating some of my grievances, so I must share his fate. A difficulty now arose, for as master professed to be a Christian, he could not consistently whip without a cause, which he could not readily find, since he could not prove that I was in any way implicated in David's crime.

Still, he could not rest satisfied until I was flogged, and therefore tried every way to find fault with me, which I knowing, did my best to prevent. But all effort to please, on my part, was useless. He sent me, one very cold day, a mile from the house to cut rails. The snow was about six inches deep. I had shoes and stockings, but still, as I had no chance to warm my feet from break of day until night, my dinner being sent me, which I was obliged to eat frozen, my feet were nearly frozen, and I was completely chilled. Mr. Barber watched me the whole day, except while away at dinner, which he hastened through as fast as possible, that he might not long lose sight of me.

When it grew dark he started for the house, bidding me follow, as it was time to feed the cattle. As I was so cold, I thought I would kindle a fire and warm me before going. I did so, and then started for the house. When passing through the yard, on my way to the cow-

*5

pen, I met Mr. B. returning, he having been there waiting for me.   He, being a holy man ! did not swear directly, but said, "Confound you, where have you been ?"
accompanying the question by a blow from a four foot
stick across my head.

I tried to explain the reason of my delay, but he would
not listen, and continued beating me.   At last I caught
hold of the stick, wrenched it from his hands, struck
him over the head, and knocked him down, after which I
choked him until he was as black as I am.   When I let
him up, he ran for his gun ; but when he returned I had
fled to parts unknown to him.   I kept away about two
weeks, staying in the woods during the day, and coming
to the quarters at night for something to eat.

Mr. Barber, however, needing my services, as it was a
very busy time, told the slaves, if they saw me, to tell
me to come home, and that he would not whip me.   This
was to me a very welcome message, for I was tired of my
life in the woods, and I immediately returned home.   I
went to work, as usual, thinking all was right ; but soon
found myself very much mistaken.

I worked about three weeks, during which I accomplished six weeks labor.   One day, while busily engaged, hoeing up new ground, I saw two men coming towards me, whom I soon recognized as constables, both of
whom I well knew.   Upon approaching near me, the
constable for our district said, " John, you must come
with me."

I dropped my hoe and followed him.   When I reached
the house, I found poor David standing bound like a

sheep dumb before its shearers. We were put up stairs to await Mr. B.'s orders, who was not then ready. The rope was tied so tight around David's wrists as to stop the circulation of the blood, and give him excruciating pain. He begged to have the rope loosened, but the officer having him in charge, would not gratify him. The other constable, however, soon come and relieved him.

Mr. Barber being ready, we set off for the magistrate's office, which was about three miles from our house. David and I were tied together, his left being tied to my right hand. On the way the constable said to me, "John, I always thought you was a good negro; what have you been doing? You ought to behave so well as not to need whipping."

I replied, "I have done nothing wrong, and if I am whipped, it shall be the last time on that farm?"

"What will you do?" asked Mr. Barber. "Run away," I answered. "When we are done with you, you will not be able to run far," said he. "Well sir, if you whip me so that I am unable to walk, I can do you no good; but if I can walk, I will take the balance of the year to myself, and go home to my mistress, at Christmas."

He did not relish this kind of talk, for he did not wish to pay my wages and not have my service, so he told me to shut my head or he would break it. Of course I said no more.

We soon arrived at the dreaded place, and were left seated in the piazza awaiting our trial, a constable being present to watch us. I asked him for a drink of water, when he said, "Would you not like a glass of brandy?"

a drink very acceptable on such occasions. I replied in the affimative, when he brought out a half-
pint tumbler nearly full, of which I drank the whole.
This roused my courage, and I felt brave. My expected
punishment was not half as much dreaded as before.

The court being ready, we were brought before his
honor, Justice Barber, uncle to my master. David was
first tried, declared guilty, and sentenced to have 39 lashes well laid upon his bare back.

My case was next in order, but Mr. Barber, instead of
preferring any charge against me, told the Judge he
would forgive me this time, as he thought I would do
better in future. Upon this the old man, raising his
spectacles and looking at me, said, " Do you think you
can behave, so as not to have to be brought before me
again ?" " Yes sir," I answered quickly. " Well sir,"
he said, " go home to your work, and if you are brought
before me again, I will order the skin all taken from your
back !"

The rope was taken off my hands, and I was told to
go in peace and sin no more. I waited to see the fate of
poor David. He was taken to the whipping post, strung
up until his toes scarce touched the ground, his back
stripped and whipped until the blood flowed in streams
to the ground. When he was taken down he staggered
like a drunken man. We returned together, talking over
the matter on the way. He said, " O, I wish I could
die ! I am whipped for no fault of my own. I wish I
had killed him, and been hung at once ; I should have
been better off." I felt sorry for him.

I determined then, if he struck me again, I would kill him. I expected another attack, and accordingly planned where I would conceal his body, where it would not readily be found, in case no one saw me perform the act. But God overruled. He had his destiny fixed, and no mortal could resist it,—no mortal arm could stay his mighty purpose. But I must hasten to the close of the year.

Mr. Barber had a most luxuriant crop of tobacco nearly ripe and ready for the harvest. Tobacco is so delicate a plant, that it will not stand the frost, and if exposed to it is thereby rendered nearly useless. Our crops had all been gathered except two fields, when by a sudden change in the wind to the north, it became so cold as to threaten a frost, which would probably destroy the tobacco remaining in the field. Mr. Barber feared this, and notwithstanding it was the Sabbath, ordered his slaves to go and secure the remainder of the crop.

Soon all hands were in the field at work. No other farmer in the neighborhood went out, all, excepting Mr. B. being willing to trust their crops to Him who had given them; although many had larger quantities exposed. Being angry with the great Omnipotent for this threatening arrangement of his providence, Mr. Barber fell to beating his slaves on the Lord's day. But his suspected enemy did not come; his fears were groundless. The night cleared off warm, and no frost came.

"God moves in a mysterious way,
"His wonders to perform;

" He plants his footsteps in the sea,
" And rides upon the storm.
" Deep and unfathomable mine
" Of never failing skill;
" He treasures up his bright design,
" And works his sovereign will.
" Ye fearful saints, fresh courage take;
" The clouds ye so much dread
" Are big with mercy, and shall break
" With blessings on your head.

" Judge not the Lord with feeble sense,
" But trust him for his grace;
" Behind a frowning providence
" He hides a smiling face.
" His purposes will ripen fast,
" Unfolding every hour;
" The bud may have a bitter taste,
" But sweet will be the flower.
" Blind unbelief is sure to err,
" And scan his works in vain;
" God is his own interpreter,
" And he will make it plain."

We worked until midnight on Sunday, and secured all
the crops, as Mr. B. thought.

The manner of curing tobacco is, to hang it up in the
barn, and put a hot fire under it, so as to cure it gradually.   But the heat must be in proportion to the damp-
ness of the tobacco.

All things being regulated, Mr. B. began to boast of
the security of his great crops.   The following Saturday, at three o'clock, P. M., he told his slaves that they
might have the remainder of that day to compensate for
the previous Sabbath, when they had worked.

The same day, while preparing to go to confession, as

usual, one of the slaves ran in and told him that the barn was on fire! I looked from the kitchen door, saw the smoke bursting from the roof, and ran to the spot. Master got there before me, and within three minutes all the slaves were upon the spot; but seeing it would be of no avail, they did not attempt to enter the barn.

Mr. Barber, moved by his usual ambition, rushed in, notwithstanding the slaves tried to persuade him of the danger, and plead with him to desist; but, blinded by the god of this world, he would not listen to their entreaties, and rushed in just as the roof was ready to fall! When they beheld the awful sight, the wails of the slaves might have been heard fully two miles.

He was caught by the end of the roof only, as it fell, from which, in a minute or two, he made his escape, his clothes all on fire. He was taken to the house, but died the next Sunday week.. Before he died, however, like Nebuchadnezzar of old, he acknowledged that God reigns among the kingdoms of men.

This sad event transpired in the month of October, after which nothing more worthy of note occurred while I remained in the family, which was until Christmas. After this I returned to my mistress, who gave me a note permitting me to get myself another home.

CHAP. X.

I now called to see a Mr. James Burkit, who had formerly been very rich, but who, by dissipation, had spent

all his property, and become quite poor. He was willing
to hire me, and sent word to my mistress to that effect.
I commenced work there on the first day of January.

There were but few slaves upon this plantation, upon
which every thing seemed in an unprosperous condition ;
fences broken down and fields overrun with weeds. I
went to work, and soon had things in better order, which
so much pleased my employer, that he made me foreman
on the plantation.

The father of Mr. Burkit, who died when James was
very young, was a very rich man, and had the reputation
among the slaves, of having been a very good master,
and of having freed a portion of his slaves at his decease, one family of whom I knew. The balance of his
slaves was divided among his heirs.

One of these freed slaves, by name George Nichols,
was a very delicate young man, unfit for field labor, and
therefore brought up waiter in the old man's family.
George being an expert hand at his business, was hired
out to a man in Washington city, where he was when his
old old master died, and where he had been for several
years previous.

As soon as the father died, his heirs tried to break the
will, and thus again enslave those who had thereby been
set free. Mr. Burkit was especially recommended to
sell George immediately, as he had been so long out of
the state, that, according to the laws of Maryland, he
was free already, independent of the will. To accomplish this, Mr. Burkit hastened directly to Washington,
and went to a hotel kept by Mr. Brown, where George

lived, whom he desired to see. George was at work in a distant part of the house, but upon receiving the message that some one wished to see him, he hastened to the bar-room, where he was both surprised and pleased to see his master James. "How *do* you do, Master James?" he inquired, smilingly, and reached out his hand to grasp that of his young master.

"I am well, how do you do, George?" was the reply.

"Very well, I thank you, sir," said poor George, and began to inquire for his parents, whom he had not seen for several years. They were very well, Mr. B. said, and then added, "George, I am about to be married, and have come for you to go to Halifax to serve as waiter at my wedding."

At this George was much pleased, thinking it highly complimentary that his young master had come so far for him, to serve at the wedding.

When Mr. Burkit made known to Mr. Brown, the hotel keeper, that he intended to sell George far south, that gentleman was much surprised, and said, "Why, Mr. Burkit, you don't mean to take George from me at this time; you will ruin me. Congress is in session, my house is full of boarders, and he is my best waiter; I cannot well get along without him. If you wish to sell him, I will buy, and give you as much for him as you can get elsewhere."

But Mr. Burkit would not sell him to Mr. Brown. George heard and knew nothing of this conversation. When he was ready, he came to the bar-room with his bundle of clothes under his arm, and soon started

off with his master James.   Mr. Brown called the latter
back and said, " Mr. Burkit, I will give you one hundred
dollars more than any other man for George ; or I will
give you eight hundred now.   No other man will give as
much, for one unacquainted with him would not give
over six hundred.   To look at him, he appears like a
very delicate boy, and indeed, he is fit only for a waiter ;
consequently worth more to a person in my business,
than to a planter.   As I know what he can do, I will
give more than a stranger would."   To all these offers
Mr. Burkit turned a deaf ear, and again started off.

On account of his tender feet, George had to wear soft
slippers, suitable only to be worn within doors.   On the
way to the vessel, which was waiting to receive them,
George said, " Master James, will you please to get me
another pair of slippers?   These I have on will be unfit
to wear at your wedding."   " O yes, George, you shall
have a pair," was the reply.

After they got on board the vessel, George said, "master James, you have forgotten my slippers."   " G—d
d—n you, if you ask for slippers, I will break your d—n
head !" was his only answer.   Then George knew, for the
first time, that he was to be sold.   His master continued,
" you have been a gentleman in Washington long enough,
now if you ask me for anything, I will beat out your
d—d brains with a handspike !"   George now felt that
his case was hopeless.

The vessel soon arrived in port, when George was put
in irons, and confined in a slave pen among a drove of
slaves, in New Market.   This dreadful news was
ge

sent to his mother, who lived at a considerable distance, but who hastened at once to see and bathe in tears her child.

When she reached the pen, she was conducted up stairs to a room, in the middle of which was a long staple driven into the floor, with a large ring attached to it, having four long chains fastened to that. To these were attached shorter chains, to which the slaves were made fast by rings around their ankles. Men, women and children were huddled in this room together, awaiting the arrival of more victims, as the drove was not full.

In this miserable condition did Mrs. Nichols, who had served out her time, find her son ; who was as much entitled to his freedom as she was to hers. And in this condition she left him forever ! Would that the Rev. Dr. Adams and others, who paint slavery in such glowingly beautiful colors, could have seen this, and have heard the agonizing cries of that mother and child, at parting ! Think of these things, ye men of God!

The trader told the poor mother, that if she could find any one to buy her son, he would sell him for just what he gave, five hundred dollars, as he was not what he wanted, and he only bought him to gratify Mr. Burkit. He continued, " I want only strong able-bodied slaves, as the best can only live five or six years at longest, and your son, being so delicate, I shall get little for him."

George then said, " Mother, don't grieve for me, it is for no crime that I have done ; it is only because I was to be free. But if you will please send to Washington, as soon as possible, and ask Mr. Brown, the gentleman that

I lived with, to buy me, I know he will gladly do so. Tell him I have one hundred and fifty dollars in my trunk, in my room at the hotel, which he can use towards paying for me."

The old woman hastened from New Market, which lies on the eastern shore of Maryland, between Cambridge and Vienna, to her own home, a distance of fifteen miles. Upon reaching home, she hastened to a friend, as she thought, (though he wore a friendly face, and possessed an enemy's heart,) to whom she related her sad story, requesting him to write for her to Mr. Brown at Washington, which he promised to do. She supposed he had done so, and waited anxiously for an answer; but none ever came, and the poor young man was carried away, where he has never since been seen or heard from by his heart-broken mother. The name of this supposed friend was Annalds. He was an old man, and a member of the Methodist church. Of course the colored people had great confidence in him, on account of his supposed piety, as he made loud professions, and talked high of heaven. But it was all hypocrisy, God in the face, and the devil in the heart; for he cheated the poor free blacks out of their rightful wages whenever he got a chance.

The plantation adjoining Mr. Burkit's was owned by a very rich planter, Robert Dennis, Esq. He was a very kind master, always treated his slaves well, would neither whip them himself, nor suffer another person to do so, and would not sell them. Consequently, he was much beloved by his slaves, who regarded him as a father.

He had a great number of well looking slaves, men,

women and children, over whom he would have no overseer, but trusted all to them in cultivating his large
tracts of land; nor did they ever betray his trust or give
him any trouble. But at length happened a sad event
to these slaves, at the death of their much beloved master. Sorrow now filled their hearts, and spread a gloom
over the whole plantation; for now, like other slaves, they
must be separated and sold from their friends and fami-
lies, some, perhaps, to cruel masters. They knew the
estate was somewhat in debt, and expected to have to be
sold to cancel it, at least part of them.

This would have been done but for Miss Betsey, who
could not endure the idea of seeing her grandfather's devoted slaves sold to pay debts which they had no hand
in contracting. She watched for an opportunity, when,
unseen by the white people, she could go to the slaves'
quarters; and having found one, she immediately hastened there, and told them that she had some bad news for
them, but dared not communicate it until they pledged
themselves not to betray her, which they readily did, as
they did not wish to bring harm upon her, which they
knew they should do by telling of her.

She then told them that there was some dispute about
the settlement of the estate, which, it was thought, could
not be settled without selling them all; which, she said,
she could not bare to see done.

They all exclaimed at once, "What shall we do?"
She answered frankly, "You had better make your
escape." They said they knew not where to go, nor how
to do. She told them that their Christmas holidays

*6

were near at hand, when they would have permission to go to visit their friends and relatives. She recommended them then to obtain of their master John, passes for this purpose, each of which was to be for a different direction from the others. Then leave for the free States.

Most of them did as she directed, obtained their passes, left for the free States, and have not since been seen at their old home.

Miss Betsey in this performed a good deed, yet she was soon after betrayed, and that, too, by a slave. An old woman, whose sons escaped with the rest, made a terrible fuss, crying and lamenting to a great rate, and saying that Miss Betsey had sent all her children off to the " Jarsers "; (meaning New Jersey, which was the only free State of which she seemed to have any idea,) and she should never see them again. She continued in this way until it came to the ears of the white people, who inquired of Miss Betsey about it. She denied all knowledge of the matter, and said, " Cousin John, do you think I would advise the slaves to run away? I have said nothing to them about being sold. Old Priss, you know, is always drunk, and knows not what she says."

This partially quieted the heirs, but did not remove all suspicion, and they still thought that Miss Betsey was in some way concerned in the affair. So when the estate was divided, they did not give her as much as would wrap around her finger, and she lived a poor girl for several years.

Subsequently she removed to Baltimore, where she

married a poor man. But God remembered her. Each of the blacks whom she helped to escape from bondage, upon hearing of her poverty, and her place of residence, sent her fifty dollars, eight hundred dollars in all, as a token of their thankfulness and gratitude.

Those who did not leave, according to her direction, were all sold.

CHAP. XI.

I WAS next hired out to Mr. Hughes, who was, comparatively, a poor man, having but one working slave of his own; the rest on his farm being all hired. His accommodations for his workmen were good; we all ate at the kitchen table.

I had not been long at this place, before it became known that I could read and write, upon which I was forbidden to visit the slaves on any of the neighboring plantations. One man, who had several pretty girls upon his farm, that I was fond of visiting, as soon as he learned that I was sometimes there, tried to catch me to whip me. But I always managed to elude him, and yet to have him know that I had been there, after I had gone away.

This provoked him most desperately, and determined him to catch me at any rate. So he employed the patrollers to watch for me, catch me if possible, and by all means bring me to him before flogging me, that he might enjoy the pleasure by sharing in it. For a long time their efforts proved unavailing. I was often in his house, in the room adjoining that in which he then was, and while the patrollers were searching the quarters.

At last, however, fortune seemed to favor him. One night, at an unusually early hour for the patrollers to be abroad, I was at one of his slave quarters, while the patrollers were at the other. One of the girls ran and told me of this, and said farther, that they would be down there soon. This, you may well guess, was no very pleasant news to me, especially as I was at the time cozily seated beside a pretty young lady. And as ladies you know, love bravery, so I did not like to hasten my usual steps, lest it should appear like cowardice; still, I knew delays were dangerous.

I considered a moment, and finally started, thinking it my safest course ; but I had not proceeded more than five feet from the door, before the enemy were upon me. There was another colored man in the quarter at the same time, who, if caught, was as liable to be whipped as myself; still, I was their special object of pursuit, as Mr. Bowlding had promised them twenty-five dollars, if they caught me on his place.

When we saw the patrollers, we both started at full speed, Ben, the other colored man, being about fifty yards ahead, and they after us. They continued the chase about a quarter of a mile, after which they returned ; but, still thinking them at my heels, I continued my flight a mile, Ben still in advance. As soon as I discovered that we were alone, I called to Ben to stop ; but he, thinking it was the voice of one of his pursuers, only put on more steam, until, finally, he ran against a rail fence, (the night being very dark,) knocked down two lengths of it, and fell upon it himself, which stopped his career until I came up, explained all, and banished his fears.

We stopped awhile to rest ourselves, and consult upon our farther course. I concluded best for me to go home, but he decided upon returning to the quarters, thinking the patrollers would now be gone, and he did not like to forego a pleasant chat with the ladies, especially as he had come so far for that express purpose. He thought this step would efface from the ladies' minds this appearance of his cowardice, and restore his reputation for heroism, because no person is allowed to possess gentlemanly bravery and valor at the South, who will run from the face of any man, or will not even courageously look death in the face, with all its terrors. I did not for a moment doubt that the company of ladies was pleasant, and that a display of heroism was a pretty sure pathway to their favor; still, I thought the preservation of a sound back, was not a thing to be overlooked, or treated lightly, so I determined to proceed homeward, which determination, as the sequel will show, proved a wise one. Ben returned to the quarters, and while standing in the yard, rehearsing the particulars of his flight, the patrollers suddenly came upon him, and seized him behind by the collar of his jacket. This garment being loose, he threw his arms back and ran out of it. And now followed another chase, in which, as before, Ben was victorious, and reached home in safety.

The affair passed off, and I supposed was ended, until about two weeks afterwards, when one day, being at work near the house, I saw two horsemen ride up to the stile, dismount and enter the house. Very soon Mr. Hughes came to the door, and requested me to come to the house. I did so, when, to my surprise, I found the horsemen were constables.

Mr. Hughes, turning to me, said, "John, these gentlemen have come to take you before a magistrate, to testify to what you know concerning the wheat that was found at Mr. Bowlding's, on the night that you ran from there." I replied, "I know nothing of the wheat, as I saw and heard of none." "Well," he said, "you will only be required to tell of what you know. Do you know the consequence of taking a false oath?"

"Yes, sir," I replied. "Well, what is it?" he asked. "I shall go to hell," I answered. "Yes, and that is not all," he said, "you will also have your ears cropped."

Turning to the constable, he said, "Mr. Waters, please send him home as soon as you are through with him, for I am very busy and need him." He added, to me, "hurry home as soon as they get done with you; do you hear?" "Yes sir," I answered. Upon this we started.

We had to go about a mile, mostly through the woods, and they, fearing I would seize this opportunity, so good a one, to try to escape, began to cut jokes to amuse me. But I had no idea of trying to escape, as I did not expect a whipping, knowing that, although a constable may seize and flog a slave, if caught from home after nightfall without a pass; still, according to law, they have no right to take him before a justice and whip him for being from home at any time, that being exclusively the master's or overseer's privilege. So I went on cheerfully.

When I reached the place of trial, I saw a large collection of people, it being the day for magistrates' meetings, and among the rest, the girl I was courting, brought there for the purpose of humbling my pride, and mortifying me. For you must think, reader, that it would be rather mortifying to be stripped and flogged in the presence of a girl, especially, after cutting such a swell as I had. Many of the crowd came expressly to see me whipped, for they thought I assumed too much of the gentleman.

Ben's case came on first, but neither of us were allowed to be present, but were kept in the yard during the trial and giving the sentence. Although, in the North it is customary to have a defendant present, to hear his case stated, yet, we were denied this, and were only informed of our sentence, after it had been passed.

Ben's sentence was to receive ten stripes, five for his first, and as many for his second offence. While being whipped, he dropped his handkerchief, which the constable picked up and handed to him, upon which he exclaimed, "D—n the handkerchief." This being reported to the justice, five stripes more were added to his first sentence, thus, making fifteen in all.

I was next brought forward, to receive five stripes, when I saw several smile, and heard them say to the constable, "Put it on well!" I was stretched up and fastened to the limb of a tree, just so that my toes could touch the ground. Every stroke buried the lash in my flesh.

When I was released, instead of returning to Mr. Hughes', I went to see my mistress, she being then at her brother Richard's. I arrived there about eight o'clock in the evening, went into the kitchen, and told the servant that I wanted to see mistress; who, upon hearing of it, came directly out, and expressed much joy at seeing me, saying : " How do you do, John?" I told her that I was almost dead. " What is the matter?" she inquired. I answered, " I am whipped almost to death." " By whom?" she asked. " By the constable, before the magistrate." " For what?" said she. I then related to her the whole story.

She rushed into the house, and told her brother of the affair, who sent for me to come in and repeat the story again to him. I did so, and also pulled off my jacket, and showed them my shirt, wet with blood. This so affected my mistress, that she commenced walking the floor, and weeping, saying meanwhile, that she was imposed upon, because she was a lone girl, and had no one to take an interest in her affairs; that if her father was alive, they would sooner thrust their heads into the fire, than treat her so. She did not believe this was for any fault of mine, but simply because they grudged her her property.

This roused master Richard at once, for when she spoke of her father, and her lonely condition, it touched him in a tender point. Now it will be recollected, that this man was a lawyer, and he was feared rather than respected by most who knew him. He bade me go home, but told me not to go to work until he came. I went home and to bed, pretending to be very sick, so that when Mr. Hughes called next morning for me to go to work, I was unable to get up. About 10 o'clock master Richard, mounted upon a fine horse, rode up, and asked to see Mr. Hughes. This gentleman immediately came out, and invited him to alight and enter the house, which invitation was declined, as, he said, all his business could be transacted there.

He inquired if Mr. Hughes knew how cruelly I had been beaten, and received for answer that he did not. That he only knew that two constables came there, bringing a warrant to take me before a magistrate, in relation to some wheat that had been found at Mr. Thomas Bowlding's.

Master Richard inquired the names of the constables and magistrates, and whatever else Mr. Hughes knew concerning the matter; after which he asked for me. Upon being called, I went out, when master Richard told me to go over to the magistrate's, which I did, reaching there before he did.

When he entered the office, he asked to see the justice's docket or books, which were shown him; but the magistrate seeing me, suspected something wrong, and commenced explaining before being asked. Master Richard said nothing, until he had finished examining the documents, where, failing to find any charge, he inquired what was the complaint alleged against me.

Oh! he said, there was no regular complaint; but Mr. Hughes said I would not work and attend to my duty at home, and Mr. Bowlding complained that I went to his plantation and kept the girls up all night, so that they were unfit for service next day ; so he thought he would order me a few stripes, just to frighten and keep me in order.

"That, then, is all, sir?" inquired master Richard, contemptuously. He then bade me take off my shirt, and exhibit my bruised back, after which he added to the justice, "Now, sir, please look at his back! is that merely to frighten him? You had no right to do this, and I will make it cost you more than he is worth!"

In the meantime, the constable came up, upon seeing whom, master Richard went towards him, asking, "Why did you whip my sister's negro in such a manner?" "Because it was my duty," was the answer. "Then, sir, it is my duty to give you just such an one," said master Richard, at the same time drawing his pistol, cocking and presenting it to the affrighted constable. "And," he continued, "I will blow out your brains, if you move!" He then, with his horsewhip, lashed the constable as much as he thought he needed, the fellow making not the least resistance.

I went home to Mr. Hughes' as well as ever, nor was I again troubled by patrollers, while I remained in his employ. He one day said to me, "John, now I hope you will stay at home. You have caused more disturbance in the neighborhood, than any one before; have caused Mr. Simpson to be turned out of office, and to be obliged to pay more than you are worth. I would not have you another year as a gift, and shall be glad when your time is up." So at Christmas, I left Mr. Hughes, and went to a new place.

CHAP. XII.

MY new master's name was Mr. Horken. He was a tolerably good man, so far as whipping was concerned; but fed his slaves most miserably, giving them meat only once each month.

At the plantation where I lived two years previously, I became acquainted with three slaves, who had now determined to make an effort to gain their freedom, by starting for the free States. They came down to see me, and try to induce me to go with them, they intending to start in about three weeks; but they exacted from me a promise of secrecy in regard to the whole matter. I had not as yet fully made up my mind to make an attempt for my freedom, therefore did not give a positive promise to accompany them. I had known several, who, having made the attempt, had failed, been brought back, whipped, and then sold far to the South. Such considerations somewhat discouraged me from making the attempt.

As the time drew near for them to start, they came again to know my decision. I told them that I had consulted my mother, whose fears for my success were so great, that she had persuaded me not to go. These three friends were very religious persons, one of them being a

Methodist preacher. He, in particular, urged me very strongly to accompany them, saying that he had full confidence in the surety of the promises of God, who had said that heaven and earth should pass away, before one jot of his word should fail; that he had often tried God, and never knew him to fail; consequently he believed he was able to carry him safely to the land of freedom, and accordingly he was determined to go. Still I was afraid to risk myself on such uncertain promises; I dared not trust an unseen God.

This visit to me was on Sunday, and they had planned to start the Saturday night following, and travel the next Sunday and Monday. It was not uncommon for slaves to go away on Saturday and not return until the following Tuesday, feigning sickness as an excuse, though this pretence not unfrequently subjected them to a flogging. So that very little alarm was felt for a slave's absence until Wednesday, unless his previous conduct had excited suspicion.

On the night on which they intended to start, accompanied by several of their fellow slaves, they repaired to an open lot of ground. Others, prompted by curiosity, followed, until quite a large concourse was assembled. Here they knelt in prayer to the great God of Heaven and Earth, invoking Him to guard them through every troublesome scene of this life, and go with them to their journey's end. Afterwards they sang a parting hymn, bidding their companions no other farewell, the hymn being exactly appropriate to the occasion. It was one of the old camp-meeting songs :—

"Farewell my dear brethren, I bid you farewell!
I am going to travel the way to excel;
I am going to travel the wilderness through,
Therefore, my dear brethren, I bid you adieu!

The thought of our parting doth cause me to grieve,
So well do I love you; still you I must leave;
Though we live at a distance, and you I no more see,
On the banks of old Canaan united we will be."

I well remember the evening of their departure. It was a beautiful night, the moon poured a flood of silver light, and the stars shone brilliantly upon their pathway, seeming like witness of God's presence, and an encouragement that he would guide them to their journey's end.

After they had gone, I began to regret that I had so much distrusted God, and had not accompanied them, and these regrets weighed so heavily upon my mind, that I could not rest day or night.

Wednesday came, and with it uproar and confusion, for three slaves were missing, of whom no one could give any account. Search was instantly made, which was, of course, unavailing, since they were already safe in some free State. Who would have thought that those contented negroes would have left their masters, preferring freedom to slavery? But they are in Canada.

Some time after this, master Richard concluded to sell his plantation, and with his slaves remove to Mississippi, my mistress consenting that he might take hers also. So he, one day, told me that I could have my choice, go with him or be sold. I told him I would not leave him to go to any one else in the known world. He then said that

7*

he would hire me out the next year, upon conditions that my employer should release me to him whenever he called for me. So when my year with Mr. Horken was up, I was hired to Dr. Johns upon the above conditions.

It was rumored about that I had given the three escaped slaves passes, it being known that I could write a tolerable hand. But master Richard looked into the affair, and finding no evidence against me, the subject was dismissed.

I lived with Dr. Johns from the commencement of the year, until the middle of June. About this time two more slaves attempted to escape, but were overtaken, caught, and brought back. It was said they had passes, but of the truth of this I am not sure, as the slaveholders reported many stories to implicate me in guilt. But God fought my battle.

To make matters appear still more in my disfavor, one slave, whom I never knew, told his master that I was going to run away, and had been trying to persuade him to go ; that my master was going to remove me South, but that I intended to leave for the free States.

These were facts; but how this slave came by them I never knew, as I had only confided them to one man, and he came off with me. I left home on Saturday night, and on Sunday several slaves were arrested and put in irons, suspected of intentions of trying to escape with me. I was about three miles from home, and knew nothing of all this, though they were hunting for me.

I felt very melancholy all day Sunday, yet knew not the cause. Early Monday morning, the constables were at Dr. Johns', waiting my arrival, to take me; but I did not go home that morning, nor have I ever since been there. Still, it was my intention to have gone, but God overruled that intention by a better.

I started early on Monday to return to the doctor's, and got within a mile of that place, to a fork of the roads, when suddenly my steps were arrested, and a voice seemed to say, don't go any farther in that direction. I stopped, considered a moment, and concluded that it was mere fancy or conceit. So I started on again; but the same feelings returned with redoubled force.

What can all this mean? I queried within myself; these sensations so strange and unusual; yet so strong and irresistable? It was God, warning me to avoid danger by not going home. So I turned upon my footsteps, and immediately these feelings left me. I sat down by the side of the road to reason upon the matter, when, for the first time, I felt an entire confidence in God, and prayed in faith.

I now made a third attempt to go home. But upon reaching the same spot, I was more uncontrollably effected than before. I became nearly blind, my head swam, and I could scarcely stand. I now felt satisfied that it was the working of an unseen God, and really think that had I still persisted in my attempts to go forward in that direction, I should have fallen as one dead, in the road.

I therefore went into the woods and stayed until night, when I went to a neighboring slave's quarters, where I got something to eat. After this, I started for Mr. Morton's plantation, where Uncle Harry's wife lived, and which was near Dr. Johns'. Harry was a carpenter, and was at work for the doctor, therefore I knew that I could learn through him the whole state of affairs there, as he came home to stay nights.

As soon as I entered the house, Uncle Harry exclaimed, "John, what have you been doing?"   "Nothing," I answered.   He then said, "the whole plantation, at the doctor's, is in an uproar about you, as they say you have been giving passes to slaves, to help them run away, which you also intend to do yourself; and, accordingly, the constables have been on the watch for you these two days.   I saw your old mother to-day, who was running from one road to the other, to meet you, to prevent your coming home, lest they should catch you.   Now I don't know what you will do, as they have advertised you, offering three hundred dollars for your arrest; so the patrollers will be looking for you; consequently you had better not stop here long.   I promised your mother to try and see you to-night."

He told his wife to give me something to eat, but told me it would not be safe for me to stay there to eat it.   I moved slowly away, but he hastened my footsteps, as did the angel those of good old Lot, for surely danger was at my heels.

Now my morning's feelings were fully explained.   I knew it was the hand of God, working in my behalf; it was his voice warning me to escape from the danger towards which I was hastening.   Who would not praise such a God?   Great is the Lord, and greatly to be praised.

I felt renewed confidence and faith, for I believed that God was in my favor, and now was the time to test the matter. About two rods from Uncle Harry's house I fell upon my knees, and with hands uplifted to high heaven, related all the late circumstances to the Great King, saying that the whole world was against me without a cause, besought his protection, and solemnly promised to serve him all the days of my life. I received a spiritual answer of approval; a voice like thunder seeming to enter my soul, saying, I am your God and am with you; though the whole world be against you, I am more than the world; though wicked men hunt you, trust in me, for I am the Rock of your Defence.

Had my pursuers then been near, they must have heard me, for I praised God at the top of my voice. I was determined to take him at his word, and risk the consequences.

I retired to my hiding place in the woods until the next night, when I returned to Uncle Harry's, that I might see or hear from my mother. I found her there waiting for me. She had brought food in her pocket for me.

I inquired if the patrollers had been there in search of me, and was told that they had not as yet, but would, doubtless, be there that night.

My mother appeared almost heart-broken. She did not wish me to go away, and had been to master Richard about me, who had promised to inquire into the accusations against me, and if there was not sufficient proof to substantiate them, they could not injure me. But he recommended that I should keep out of sight for the present, and if he could do nothing else in my favor, he would so manage, that when he was ready to go South, I could be got off with him. I thought this a very wise plan too, in case I desired to go South; but I had fully resolved to go North.

I did not, however, communicate this resolution to mother, as I saw she was not in a proper condition to receive it. She promised to go again to master Richard, and come and let me know the result of her visit. But I knew I should never again see her, and that I was then probably taking my last look of her—this side the grave.

Upon leaving me, she took my hand, and in a voice choked by sobs, gave me her parting blessing. My heart was so full that I could scarcely endure this, and but for the support of God, I must have fainted. I now returned to my hiding place, leaving word with Uncle Harry, where the friend who had promised to come away with me, might find me.

As soon as he heard he came directly to see me, for he had been anxious lest I should go off without him.

CHAP. XIII.

THIS friend lived about eight miles from my hiding place, to which he walked after his day's work was ended. He wished me to go home and stay with him until he was ready to leave. I was very glad to do this, as he had a secure place, where they would least expect to find me. We had appointed two different times before this to start, and had been disappointed; still, his determination was firm to go.

I left my old hiding place, where I had spent one comfortable week, in solemn meditation and sweet communion with God, and went home with my friend.

He was coachman to his master, and had a room above the kitchen, which no one entered but himself, and where he concealed me. His master drove, whipped, and clothed his slaves most unmercifully, but fed them uncommonly well; consequently, my friend was able to feed me well, while I was his guest, he often coming to his room unseen, to see if I needed any thing.

He went one night to the neighborhood where I had lived, but returned with very discouraging news. Three hundred dollars had been offered for me, and I had been advertised in all the papers; therefore, he thought my way so much hedged in, that my escape was impossible, and finally concluded not to try himself. I did not care so much for the advertisement, as for this determination of his, which rather discouraged me, for I knew he was a shrewd man, also, that his business had often taken him from home in different directions; therefore, I thought he would know more of the way than myself, and I had accordingly, waited long for, and relied much upon, him. But my trust in Him who will not forsake in time of need, was greater; so I resolved to try the road alone and abide the consequences.

I passed most of my time in supplication to my Great Conductor, until the next Friday, the time appointed for my departure. The most discouraging thing seemed my ignorance of the direction I ought to pursue. I knew well that dangers thickly beset the pathway, and that should I miss my way, it would be almost certain failure to inquire it of a white man; also, that I must starve rather than ask one for food.

Various were the suggestions which the enemy of souls continually presented to my mind, to weaken my trust in God; but, like Abraham of old, I drove them away, still held my confidence, and prayed incessantly. The all-important Friday now came, and I thought it necessary to make one more trial, a third covenant with God, since it is said a threefold cord is not easily broken. So I again inquired of Him relative to this undertaking, and was soon spiritually convinced that He was still with me, and would so continue to the end of my journey; so I fully and finally committed myself to his charge, and determined to start that night.

About three o'clock in the afternoon my friend came in with the good tidings that he had changed his mind, and concluded to accompany me, which quite encouraged me, though it did not change my trust from divine to human aid. The evening came, and with it my friend, true to his promise. He said, " Come, let us be going; I believe God's promise is sufficient, and I will try Him, and see what He will do for me. Let us trust everything to him and serve him better. If we are taken, he has power to provide a way for our escape."

We started about 8 o'clock in the evening. After travelling about three miles, we saw many horses feeding near the road, and concluding that four legs were better adapted to speed than two, we took one apiece. We went to a barn and took two blankets, but while hunting for bridles, were routed and chased some distance by the faithful watch dogs of the farm. Then we concluded to go to nature's manufactory ; so we cut grape vines, made for ourselves bridles, mounted our horses, and rode at full speed until day-break, after which we turned them loose, leaving them to shift for themselves, and thanking them for their aid to us. I think we must have travelled at least forty miles that night ; yet, strange to say, did not meet a single person.

The following day we travelled rapidly, and, about four o'clock, P. M., reached Washington city. I went to a store and bought a pair of shoes, and on the way met a colored man with whom I was acquainted, we having been raised on the same farm. He inquired what wind blew me there at that time of year, it not being holiday time. I knew this man was a Christian, and therefore that it was safe to trust him, which is not true of all, since there are as many treacherous colored, as white men. I told him I had started for the free States, and thought to go to Baltimore by steamboat ; but he said that would be impossible.

I asked what I should do ; to which he replied that he could not tell, but pointing to a house near by, said, " There lives Mrs. R., a free woman, and one of God's true children, who has travelled there many times, and

can direct you.   You may depend upon what she tells
you."

I went as directed, and inquired for Mrs. R.   She invited me to enter, and asked where I was from; upon
which I related my whole history, during the recital of
which tears ran down her cheeks.   When I ended, she
said, " let us pray."   We knelt before God, when such a
prayer as I never heard from mortal lips, fell from hers.
I felt God's presence sensibly.

After the prayer was concluded, she gave us a very
good dinner.   I asked for pen and ink, and prepared to
write a pass, upon which she said, " Lay aside those earthly, selfish dependencies ; God cannot work when you depend partly on self; you must put your trust entirely in
Him, believing him to be all-sufficient.   If you will do
this," she added, with raised hands, " I will give my
head for a chopping block, if he does not carry you safely through, for I never knew him to fail."

She then gave us directions for our journey, naming
the dangerous places which we were to avoid ; after which
we started with renewed courage.   After travelling about
two miles we came to a bridge, upon which were many
hands at work, under the supervision of a " boss."   They
did not address us, although they looked steadily at us,
as if they wished to do so.

This was a toll bridge, at which footmen paid two
cents, but when we crossed, the toll man was in so high
dispute with a teamster, who had just crossed, that he
did not notice us.   Thus God paid our toll.

About a mile beyond this, we came to a place where

were several Irishmen quarrying stone. They stopped work as we approached, looked hard at us, and I heard them say, " Here come two negroes who look like runaways ; we can make a penny apiece off them, let's take them up." This was a trying time, and exercised all the faith of which we were possessed. But faith is the substance of things hoped for, and the evidence of things not seen ; by it the elders obtained a good report.

But notwithstanding the suggestions of these men and our passing near them, still they did not molest us, although they followed us with their eyes, as far as they could see us. This was another Ebenezer for us to raise, in token of God's deliverance ; so when we were out of their sight, we knelt and offered up our thanksgiving to God for this great salvation.

Three miles farther on we passed a village tavern, at the door of which stood a stage coach loaded with passengers, of the driver of which we inquired the way to a certain town. We had travelled about a mile in the direction he designated, when we saw two horsemen following us, in great haste. We suspected they were in pursuit of us, but as there were no woods near, saw no means of escape.

As they came up they said, "Boys, where are you going ?" We named the town which was about three miles distant. "You will not get there to-night," said one. " No, sir, we don't expect it," I answered.

They kept along with us for about a mile. I soon suspected their object was to arrest us, that they dared not attempt it alone, but that they hoped to meet some one who would assist them. One of them entered a tavern, which we passed, but finding no help there, came out and continued on with us.

After awhile one of them rode on ahead of us, when the other tried to check him by saying, " We must not go so fast, they will take another road." This verified our suspicions that they were after us.

My companion began to complain that it was now a gone case with us, and said he wished he had not come. I reproved him for this faithlessness ; told him if this was his course of procedure, that we should soon be taken up, and reminded him of his promise to trust in God, let danger assume whatever shape it might. I told him my confidence remained unshaken, that I had no reason at all to doubt. Upon this he braved up, and went on cheerfully.

When we approached the town of Rockville, our undesirable companions road off at full speed, thinking, doubtless, that we should be foolish enough to follow. We thought it wisest, however, as soon as they were out of sight, to take the woods until night. But whilst resting under the bushes, we observed two boys approaching, one black the other white. The latter exclaimed at once, "There are two runaways, I will go and tell my father."

The boys went directly to a man who was near by ploughing, and informed against us. We saw that to remain there would be unsafe, so we resumed our journey. As we stood on a hill near Rockville, we could look down into the village, where we saw many people, apparently awaiting our arrival ; therefore we presumed the two horsemen had only gone ahead to prepare for our reception.

We saw a colored man near by, of whom we inquired what course we could take to go around the village ; but he would give us no information whatever. So we decided that our best way was to venture directly through the town, and had started to do so, when a colored man, who was driving a wood team, seeing that we were strangers, and guessing we were runaways, came near and said to us, "I see you are strangers, and I hope you will excuse my boldness in addressing you. I wish to say, that you had best not go through the village, unless you have the necessary papers. Whether you have such documents you best know. No colored man can pass here, without being subjected to a close examination."

We thanked him, and gave him to understand that we felt our cases to be nearly desperate, and wished him to tell us the best way to. go around the town. He kindly told us, and we started to follow his directions, which were to go through the woods and enter the main road again, on the other side of the town.

But we had proceeded but a little way into the wood, when, to our surprise, we saw coming towards us, down the road, a great number of men, some on foot, others on horses, who had probably seen us as we left the road for the wood. We fell back farther into the woods, but it being large timber, with few bushes, we had little chance of concealment, and were truly in a bad fix.

We at last found an old tree, which had fallen so that the trunk was supported by the limbs about two feet from

the ground.   Under this we crawled and lay flat upon
our faces, as being the safest place we could find, and little safety there seemed to me in this, for I thought a man
a hundred yards off might have seen us, with half an
eye.

We saw the huntsmen and their dogs within ten yards
of us, and even heard them say, " They must be near
this place!"   We lay still, and held God to his promise,
though when danger came so near, our hopes began to
vanish, and like Israel we began to mourn.   But stand
still and see the salvation of God, which he will show
thee to-day.

Presently one man said, " I think they have gone farther into the woods.   There is no place of concealment
here, and besides the dogs would find them."   Oh, foolish man!   God bestowed their senses and he can take
them away.   He can touch one nerve of the brain, and
directly their understanding is lost.

They finally went farther into the woods, listening to
their dogs, who seemed as anxious as their masters, to
find us; but they could not hit upon the right trail.
We remained under the friendly tree from five in the afternoon until ten in the evening; when, thinking all was
safe, after returning God our thanks, we left our hiding
place, and pursued our journey, determining to travel
hereafter no more by day.

CHAP. XIV.

ABOUT three miles farther on we discovered two horses saddled, standing tied in the wood near the road, which, we soon discovered, were the same upon which the men rode who had overtaken us before we reached Rockville. We knew them by the pieces of buffalo skin on their saddles. Their riders had evidently left them and concealed themselves near by, to watch the road, thinking we should leave our hiding places after dark, and resume our journey.

Upon making this discovery we entered a rye field, through which we passed, still keeping the road in sight. Thus we went on for two or three hours, through fields, bushes and swamps, until worn out with fatigue and hunger, we were forced to lie down to rest. Here we soon fell asleep, and did not awake until day-light. It was now Sunday. After praying we resumed our journey, taking the road.

Uncertain ourselves whether we were in the right or wrong way, we could only trust to the guidance of the Great Pilot as we travelled onward, and when we were hungry we prayed for spiritual food, which seemed to strengthen and fill us.

We now saw a colored man sitting upon the fence, about a mile from us, whom we approached, when he immediately accosted us in these words : "Good morning, my friends, I have been sitting here for about an hour, unable to move with all the effort I could make, when I ought to have been at home, (as I am a coachman,) pre-

paring my horses and carriage to take the people to
church. I now feel why I have been thus forced against
my will to remain here; it is that I may help you. And
now tell me what I can do for you, for as God liveth I
will do it if possible."

We told him that we had been travelling since Friday,
without any food, and were now nearly famishing. Pointing to a farmer's house, he said, " Go there and inquire
for my wife ; tell her I sent you that she might give you
something to eat. She is the cook for the farm.

We thanked him, and started to follow his directions.
Upon reaching the house, we saw the overseer standing
in the yard, who scrutinized us very closely and suspiciously. Nevertheless we inquired for the cook, who
soon made her appearance, when we did our errand ; and
although she quickly answered, "I don't see why he
should send you here, for I have nothing for you to eat,
and he knows it ;" still, we could see that we had awak-
ened her sympathy, and that she only answered thus in-
differently because of the overseer.

He, however, told her to give us some breakfast ; upon
which she took us into the kitchen, while he started instantly to get help to take us. The cook suspected as
much, and told us so, and the slaves immediately concealed us very carefully. Soon the overseer returned with
his help, and inquired for us, when the slaves told him
that we went away soon after he did. He inquired in
what direction, and when they had told him, he started
off in hot haste in pursuit.

The slaves expressed great astonishment that we had

come so far without getting taken up, but told us to keep still, and they would take care of us. At night a free colored man took us through unfrequented paths, to escape the vigilance of the overseer, until we reached Fredericktown, when he said he could go no further, as, if we were taken and he found in our company, it would ruin him. Moreover, he was fearful we could not get through the town, as no colored man was allowed to pass through after nightfall. Therefore, to avoid creating suspicion and being arrested, we decided to part company for the present, I to go through the town on one side, and my companion on the other.

Before parting from our kind conductor, we knelt down and besought God to conduct us on our way, and shield us from all harm ; and again we made a mutual promise, to place all our trust in divine strength. We saw many people as we passed through the town, none of whom noticed us, until we were about to leave it, when we perceived a large and noisy crowd, apparently intoxicated, coming towards us.

We left the road until they had passed, when we again resumed our journey together. We soon came to a fork in the roads, when, not knowing which to take, we pulled down a guideboard and ascertained ; after which we went on until daybreak, when we took shelter in the woods during the day on Monday.

The following night we travelled without interruption, and on Tuesday lay all day concealed in a rye field. We travelled Tuesday night until within five miles of Baltimore, when we missed our way. Here again we had an instance of God's care for us, for had the night been one hour longer, we should probably have reached Baltimore, and been taken.

But, early in the morning we met a colored man, who, as we hesitated to answer him when he asked where we were going, said we need not fear him, as he was friendly, and would not hurt a hair of our heads. Thus assured we revealed to him our secret, when he exclaimed, "My friends, you are running directly to destruction! That is the road to Baltimore, which is but five miles distant, where you will certainly fall into the hands of your enemies, who are on the sharp lookout for all such chances, therefore you had best take a different route."

We were truly alarmed, for day now broke suddenly and unexpectedly upon us, from a hitherto dark and cloudy sky. We knew not what to do, as there was no forest large enough in sight, in which to conceal ourselves, so we besought our new friend to direct us, which he did by pointing out to us a poor, dismal looking old frame in a small wood, occupied by a free colored man.

Thither we went, and were kindly received by the man's family, who gave us food, of which we were in great need. My feet and ankles were so much swollen, that we found it necessary to remain here two days, about which we felt many misgivings since the man was often intoxicated, when he was very communicative, and I feared he might unintentionally, if in no other way, betray us, for I knew no dependence could be placed on a drunken man.

Friday night we started again, the man having told us

what route to take; and that when we reached the Sus-
quehanna, we should have no other means of crossing
but to steal a boat for that purpose. The next day as
we lay concealed near the road, under the bushes, we
could hear the people converse as they passed.

We finally concluded not to go on this way any farther, as the chance of stealing a boat was a very hazardous
one, but to return to the place from whence we last started, and see if we could not obtain some better instructions. On our way back, we passed a house from which
a man hailed us with, "Hallo, boys, where are you going? stop awhile." I said we were going home, and had
no time to stop. This was about midnight.

As we heard him call his dogs, we left the road and
went through the wheat fields to the woods, where we
soon heard him pass at full speed, with his dogs. We
hastened to our friend's house, but he advised us not to
lose a moment in making our way off, as they would
most likely come to search his house, knowing him to be
a free man. He directed us by another route, which was
a very dangerous one, being watched constantly to the
borders of Pennsylvania; but told us to go to another
free colored man, six miles distant, who could perhaps
direct us better.

He cautioned us about passing a house, which he carefully described to us, in which lived a negro buyer, who
watched to catch runaways. But, notwithstanding his
caution, we unluckily found ourselves almost at the door
of his house, before we were aware of it. We however
passed it unperceived.

Early next morning we arrived at the house to which

we had been directed, and called up the owner. As soon as I heard him speak, I knew him to be a man of God, for his words betrayed him. He called his wife to come quickly and prepare food, for two wayworn and hungry travellers, which she hastened to do. Now, who told this man of our necessities? for we had not. But never refuse to entertain strangers, for some have thus entertained angels unawares.

When the table was spread ready for breakfast, the old man approaching the throne of grace, with eyes uplifted towards heaven, repeated the following hymn, which the whole family joined in singing :—

> " And are we yet alive?
> See we each other's face?
> Glory and praise to Jesus give,
> For his redeeming grace.
> Preserved by power divine,
> To full salvation here;
> Again in Jesus' praise we join,
> And in his sight appear.
> What troubles have we seen,
> What conflicts have we passed?
> Dangers without and fears within?
> Since we assembled last.
> But out of all the Lord
> Hath brought us by his love;
> And still he doth his help afford,
> And hides our lives above."

While they were singing, the mighty power of God filled my frame like electricity, so that whereas I had before been hungry and weak, I now felt the strength of a giant; I could no longer restrain my feelings.

This was Sunday morning, and the family started soon

after breakfast for the Methodist church, which was three miles distant, taking my friend and leaving me locked up in the house, for my limbs were so swollen that it was deemed advisable that I should rest during the day. Four others accompanied them on their return, towards one of whom my heart leaped for joy as soon as I saw him, for I felt that he was a servant of the Most High. He instantly grasped my hand, saying, "Have you faith in the Lord Jesus Christ?" I answered in the affirmative, when he continued, "Well, God has brought you thus far, and he will conduct you safely to the land of freedom."

After dinner and a round of prayers, we started on our way, these friends accompanying us. We were supposed to be some of their neighbors, whom, having been with them to church, they were accompanying homeward. They continued with us until dark, taking us through fields and by-paths. When they left us, they said we were within two nights' travel of the Pennsylvania line, but cautioned us against one dangerous place, which having passed, we should probably have little more to fear.

This was a large two storied white house standing near the road, about two rods from which stood a barn thatched with rye straw. The owner's business was to catch slaves, for which purpose he kept well trained dogs, who having once got on our track, would follow for miles, and the master would shoot us if we did not surrender, therefore we should be careful to avoid this place, in particular.

Our friends left us, and we went on, but before we knew it we had passed the barn, and were near the house. As soon as we perceived our mistake, we took to the fields. Everything was still about the house, until I, in attempting to get over a fence, broke down, when I made so much noise as to rouse the dogs, which presently began to bark. This brought out the master, who tried to urge them on, but, strange to say, though they ran to and fro, they could not strike our trail.

We did not venture into the public road again that night. The next day we lay by, and at eight o'clock in the evening again started, hoping to reach port before morning.

Our friends had told us, that when we reached the Baltimore turnpike, leading into Pennsylvania, that we were then over the line. About three o'clock in the morning we came to a shanty, on the edge of a wood, so small and mean that I thought no person inhabiting it would have the courage to attempt our arrest. My friend objected to going to the house, but I wanted to inquire the way, having got somewhat bewildered. So I went and knocked at the door, until a surly voice called out, " Who's there?" " A friend," I answered. " What does the friend want?" he inquired. " To know if he is on the direct road to the Baltimore turnpike, and how far it is there," I said. " Yes, go on, it is about half a mile," he said, in a voice which plainly denoted that he did not wish to be disturbed by night rovers, though a price of three hundred dollars was on the head of the one then at his door.

We pursued our course, and shortly came to the much desired turnpike, when we clasped glad hands, and went on the next mile or two, rejoicing and praising God for this deliverance. We now imagined ourselves out of danger, but were mistaken, for after passing York we came to a village called Berlin, where we were attacked by a Dutchman, who came running out of a carpenter's shop and grasped me by the shoulder, at the same time muttering over some lingo, wholly incomprehensible to me.

But I looked at him so furiously, at the same time thrusting my hand into my pocket, as if after some weapon of defence, that he became so frightened as to loose his grasp, and run backwards as if his life was in danger. I followed him to the great amusement of the by-standers, who were looking on to see him take me.

I supposed my companion was close by, but when I turned round I saw him about six rods distant, walking off at a rapid speed, and leaving me to do the best I could alone. This cowardice somewhat enraged me, but when I overtook him he so excused himself that I forgave him, knowing that his spirit was willing, but his flesh was weak.

CHAP. XV.

WE at last reached Columbia, Pennsylvania, where we intended to stop and hire out to work. But the people advised us to go on farther, as already there were two slave hunters in the place in pursuit of two fugitives, whom they had traced to that place. Accordingly we started again the following night, and after travelling about ten miles, reached the house of an elderly quaker, who offered us a home with him until he could get places for us. These he soon procured, and we went to work; and oh, how sweet the reflection that I was working for myself. We remained here about six months, when we were again routed by the arrival of slave hunters, who had already taken two women and some children, and were in pursuit of other fugitives. In consequence of this, many of the colored people were leaving this for safer parts of the country; so we concluded to go to Philadelphia.

I went first, and my friend soon followed. We had not been there many days, before he was met and recognized by a lady, in Chestnut Street; but he feigned ignorance of her, and did not answer when she addressed him. He came directly and told me of the affair, which at first gave me great alarm, but as we heard nothing more from her, our fears gradually subsided.

My friend soon married, and not long after moved to Massachusetts, whither he was driven by one day seeing his old master in one of the streets of Philadelphia, peering into the face of every colored man who happened to pass.

I soon got into bad company, and forgot the goodness of that Being who had shown me so much kindness, who had stuck by me closer than a brother, through all my wanderings, and who had finally brought me from bondage to a land of freedom. I often now reflect upon my ungratefulness towards him.

One night, while returning from my day's labor, I fell into meditation upon the past blessings of God to me. When I reached home I looked in the Bible to find something applicable to my case, when I, almost immediately, opened at Luke's Gospel, 15th chapter and 18th verse, " I will arise and go to my father."

I felt a heavy load resting upon my heart; I felt as if I had neglected the Saviour, and God had forever withdrawn his spirit from me. I knelt in prayer, and like Jacob, wrestled manfully. I continued in this state six weeks, until the meeting of the Methodist Conference, which took place in the Bethel Church, in Philadelphia. When it commenced I was sick, and had been confined to my bed two weeks. I heard people talk of the great revival, and of the excellent preaching they were having, and though I was then confined to my bed by sickness, and the rain was falling fast, still I was resolved to go to church, for I felt that my soul was at stake, and I did go, notwithstanding friends tried to prevail on me to remain at home.

I took my seat in a dark corner of the church, while the congregation were singing for their own amusement. Presently a tall man entered, went into the pulpit, and read the following hymn :

9

" Hark, my soul! it is the Lord;
It is the Saviour, hear his word;
Jesus speaks, he speaks to thee,
He says, poor sinner, love thou me.

I delivered thee when bound,
And when wounded healed thy wound;
Sought thee wandering, set thee right,
Turned thy darkness into light.

Can a woman's tender care
Cease towards the child she bare?
Yes, she may forgetful be,
But I will remember thee."

He lined the hymn so that all could sing, during which he often called the attention of the congregation to the sentiment, to all which I paid great attention, for my mind was forcibly carried back to the state of bondage from which I had just escaped, and the many manifestations of God's mercies to me throughout the journey. The hymn was not sung by wood or brass, but by mortal tongues, which were more charming in their harmony than ten thousand stringed instruments.   This hymn was so precisely suited to my case that I began to feel much better.

The preacher, Rev. Josiah Gilbert, of Baltimore, then arose, taking for his text, " O, praise the Lord, for He is good, and His mercies endure forever."   Never before nor since have I heard such a sermon.   The load was removed from my heart, and I found myself standing up in the church, praising God, for it seemed to me a heaven upon earth to my soul.

I felt nothing more of my sickness, and next day went

to my work, tending for brick-layers. The following night, at the meeting the question was put if any person wished to join the church. No person went about among the crowd to drag others to the altar, or to force them to say they had religion, when they had none; yet one hundred and twenty, like noble volunteers, forced their way to the altar, and gave in their names, shouting the praises of Immanuel's God, while the preacher was recording them.

I joined the church that same night. O, memorable night! Would that I could bring thee back, that I might live thee over again! But thou art gone, and I can only live over thy blessings in memory. But they will not so flee.

I married the same year, and for a time everything seemed to go on well. God gave me a companion who loved Him, and we soon had a family altar in our lowly habitation. Sickness and sorrow however came. Several slaves near by were arrested and taken to the South, so I finally concluded best for me to go to sea, and accordingly removed to New York city for that purpose.

MANY of my friends have expressed a curiosity to learn how I, being a slave, obtained an education; to gratify which I will now relate some incidents in my past life, which I have not done in the foregoing pages.

When about eight years of age, I was sent to the school house with the white children, to carry their dinners, it being a distance of two miles, and therefore too far for them to go home for them. There were two of these children relatives of my master, whose father had once been rich, but who, through misfortune, left his children almost penniless at his decease.

Little Henry, one of the children, was one morning, while walking leisurely to school, repeating over his lesson, when I said to him, "How I would like to read like you." "Would you?" said he, "Then I will learn you." I told him, if his Uncle knew it, he would forbid it.

"I know it," he answered, "But I will not tell him; for he would then stop you from going with me, and I would have to carry my own dinners!" Thereupon we made a mutual promise to reveal our secret to no person.

Henry was about my own age, being the elder of the two children; his sister, Jane, being about five years old. He commenced teaching me from his book my letters. We sometimes started an hour or two before school time, that we might have more leisure for our undertaking. We had a piece of woods to pass on our way, which also facilitated the practical operation of our plans, as we could, by going into them, escape the observation of the other school children, or of passers by in the road. We even sometimes took Jane to the school house, leaving her to play with the other children, while we returned to our school in the woods, until the school bell rang.

I made such rapid progress that Henry was encouraged and delighted. When my father knew of the matter, he gave Henry some money with which to purchase me a book, which he did of one of the scholars, who, being advanced into a higher lesson, had no longer use for this book.

I now lost no time, but studied my lessons every leisure moment, at all convenient times. I went thus with the children to school about three years, when I became the body servant of John Wagar, and had to give my attention to him and his horse.

John being six miles from home, at a boarding school, was only at home from Saturdays until Mondays. During his absence I had to attend to his pony, and do small jobs about the house, which did not prevent my continuing my studies, although my opportunities to do so were not now as good as formerly; still, my little teacher improved every chance that offered of giving his instructions.

I soon got through my first book, Webster's Spelling Book, after which Henry bought me the Introduction to the English Reader. He also commenced setting me copies, as he thought it time I was commencing to write, though he still kept me at reading until I had nearly completed my second book, when our school was broken up by the return of John Wagar from the boarding school, he having completed his education.

John, whose father was very rich, hardly treated Henry, a poor orphan boy, with common courtesy or decency, and was unwilling even to sit and eat with him at table. Mrs. Ashton, Henry's mother, noticed this conduct of John's, and also that his father sided with him in all his complaints against Henry, and knowing the cause she did not wish longer to remain where she was; so she,

with the children, removed to Alexandria, where Henry
is now doing a large dry goods business, in which, by
honesty and skill, he has accumulated considerable
wealth.

When Henry was about to leave the plantation, he
said to me, " I am sorry, John, that I cannot teach you
longer, as I had intended to learn you through the English Reader, and also to write a good hand. But you
must not forget what you have learned, and try to improve what you can by yourself."

This parting filled my heart with sorrow, for I loved
Henry Ashton like a brother. I followed him with my
eyes until distance closed the view ; and my affectionate
prayers and good wishes always have, and always will,
follow him, for to him I owe the rudiments of one of my
greatest blessings, my education. Through this I have
been enabled to read the Word of God, and thereby learn
the way of salvation ; and though I could never repay
these services, yet God has doubly paid him, for before I
left Maryland his name ranked among the most respectable and wealthy of country merchants.

After this I continued to read and write at every opportunity, often carrying my book in my hat, that I might
lose no chance of using it. When I was with Richard
Thomas, in the south part of the State, I became acquainted with a poor Englishman, who lived near the
plantation. He, seeing my strong desire to learn, proposed to instruct me, after exacting from me a promise of
secrecy in the matter. He continued to teach me from
the first of March until the October following, when he
and his daughter, (his whole family,) died.

After that I had no teacher until I went to Philadelphia, where I attended evening schools during the winters of my stay in that city.

CHAP. XVI.

VOYAGE TO THE INDIAN OCEAN.

WHEN I reached New York, in consequence of my inexperience I could get no berth on shipboard, as they only wanted to employ able seamen, so I was advised to go to New Bedford, where green hands were more wanted, and where, I was told, I could go free of expense.

Accordingly, next morning, in care of an agent, I started on board a vessel bound for that port. When I arrived there, I was told I could only go before the mast as a raw hand, as a great responsibility rested upon the cook, or steward, of a whaling vessel, bound upon a long voyage, one of which places I preferred and solicited.

I soon saw there was no chance for me with that master, so I went to the office of Mr. Gideon Allen, who was fitting out a ship for sea, and wanted both cook and steward. I approached him with much boldness, and asked if he would like to employ a good steward, to which he replied in the affirmative, asking me at the same time if I was one.

I told him I thought I was. So, without much parley-

ing we agreed upon the price, when he took me down to
the vessel, gave to my charge the keys of the cabin, and
I went to work as well as I knew how.

The following day the Captain, Mr. Aaron C. Luce,
come on board with Mr. Allen, who introduced me to
him as the captain of the ship, with whom I was going
to sea. The captain looked at me very suspiciously, as
much as to say, you know nothing of the duties of the
office you now fill.

At the house where I boarded was a cook, who, in consequence of deformed feet, could not obtain a berth, as
the captains and ship owners thought he would thereby
be disenabled for going aloft when necessity required it.
This man told me that if I would get him a place as
cook, he could and would give me all needful instruction
in reference to my office.

I was pleased with an offer which promised so well for
me, and accordingly recommended him to Mr. Allen for
cook, who, supposing I knew the man, and that all was
right, hired him.

The Milwood, on which we were to sail, was a splen-
did vessel, called a three boat ship. She was arranged
to carry 3500 bbls. of oil, with a crew numbering twenty-five hands, with four principal officers, captain and
three mates, and three boatswains, who are termed sub-
ordinate officers. All things being in readiness, the hands
were summoned on board, when, at the pilot's command,
she was loosed from her moorings at the dock, floated out
of the harbor, and with well filled sails, stood out to sea.

The thoughts of the voyage and of the responsibilities

which I had taken upon myself, were anything but pleasant. I knew that I was wholly ignorant of a steward's duties, and consequently expected to incur the captain's just displeasure for my assurance and imposition, since at sea every man is expected to know his own duty, and fill his own station, without begging aid from others. But again I reflected that God was all sufficient, at sea as well as upon the land, so I put my trust in him, fully confident that he would bring me out more than victorious.

As I bid my family farewell, and left the American shore, I thought over the following lines :

Jesus, at thy command,
  I launch into the deep ;
And leave my native land,
  Where sin lulls all to sleep.
For thee I would this world resign,
And sail to Heaven with thee and thine.

Thou art my pilot, wise ;
  My compass is thy word ;
My soul each storm defies,
  Whilst I have such a Lord.
I trust his faithfulness and power,
To save me in a trying hour.

Though rocks and quicksands deep,
  Through all my passage lie ;
Yet Christ will safely keep,   -
  And guide me with his eye.
My anchor, hope, shall firm abide,
And everlasting storms outride.

Soon after the pilot left us I became very sea sick, and unable to attend to my duties, which, consequently, all devolved upon the cook, he having promised to assist me. But of this he soon grew tired, and complained to the captain, hoping to get my place; so he told him I was a greenhorn, had never been to sea before, and knew nothing of a steward's office.

The captain, who had been deceived by my sickness, now came into the cabin very angry, and said to me, "What is the matter with you?" I told him I was sick.

"Have you ever been at sea before?" he asked. I told him I never had, upon which he asked how I came to ship as steward? I answered, "I am a fugitive slave from Maryland, and have a family in Philadelphia; but fearing to remain there any longer, I thought I would go a whaling voyage, as being the place where I stood least chance of being arrested by slave hunters. I had become somewhat experienced in cooking by working in hotels, inasmuch that I thought I could fill the place of steward."

This narrative seemed to touch his heart, for his countenance at once assumed a pleasing expression. Thus God stood between me and him, and worked in my defence.

He told me that had circumstances been different, he should have flogged me for my imposition; but now bade me go on deck, where I could inhale the fresh air, and I should soon be well. I did so and soon recovered.

The captain became as kind as a father to me, often going with me to the cabin, and when no one was present, teaching me to make pastries and sea messes. He had a cook book, from which I gained much valuable information.

I was soon able to fulfill my duty to the gratification and satisfaction of the captain, though much to the surprise of the whole crew, who, knowing I was a raw hand, wondered how I had so soon learned my business. But I could never suit the mate, do the best I could, for he wanted me put before the mast, and for more than four months kept a grudge against me. The cook also, disappointed in not getting my place, often complained of me to my enemy, the mate. And not satisfied with this, he had the baseness to forbid my going to the galley to look after my cooking, and it was often spoiled. But I bore all with patience, as I knew that I had two good friends, in the captain and God. This trouble was, however, soon removed, for the cook was taken sick before we reached Fayal, where he was left in charge of the American Consul, to be sent home.

When we had been about three weeks out, we captured a sperm whale, which furnished eighty-five bbls. of oil, which we sent home from Fayal, where we remained just long enough to discharge the oil, and take on board a fresh supply of water and vegetables, which required about three days.

Shortly after leaving this place, while the captain was aloft one day, the mate became so much exasperated with me as to beat me. He took hold of me, whereupon I threw him down, but did not strike him. Upon entering the cabin, the captain found me in tears, and inquired the cause. I told him that, do the best I could, I was unable to please the mate, who had been beating me now, for no cause of which I was conscious. He told me to do my duty to the best of my ability, and he would take care of the rest.

He then went upon deck, and inquired of the mate of what I was guilty deserving a flogging; who replied that I was unfit to be in the cabin, and ought to be before the mast; that I was too much of a gentleman to be at sea. Whereupon the captain told him not to lay a finger upon me again, for I was his steward, and the mate had no control over me, which he wished him, the mate, to plainly understand. The captain allowed I was green enough, but said that I was willing to do the best I knew; that when the mate first went to sea, he was as green as I was, and that every man must have a chance to learn before he could do his duty.

The mate accused the captain of partiality to me, upon which the captain gave him to understand that he was master of the vessel, and should treat each man as he deserved, from the mate to the cook. After this I soon fell in favor with the mate and all the crew. The mate was a resolute man, and a good whaleman. Being steward I was not obliged to go in the boats for whales unless I chose, or unless some one of the hands was unable to go, whose place I was to fill, of necessity.

The manner of arranging the boats in a ship of this character, is as follows: Three boats, ready fitted, are kept swinging in the cranes alongside the ship; these are called the starboard, larboard and waist boats. Each is manned by six men, including the officer, and each has its regular crew. The captain commands the starboard, the first mate the larboard, and the second mate the waist boat. The third mate commands the captain's boat, when the latter does not go.

Each boat carries five oars, the officer steering, while the harpooner, who is termed the boatswain, rows the bow oar, until the whale is fastened with the harpoon, which operation is performed by this person. This being done, the boatsteerer goes aft and takes the officer's place, while that person goes forward to kill the whale; which is done with a sharp spear, about six feet long, called a lance.

The harpoon is sharp, and barbed at one end, so that when it has once entered the animal, it is difficult to draw it out again, and has attached to its other end a pole, two inches thick and five feet long. Attached to this is a line 75 or 100 fathoms in length, which is coiled into the bow of the boat. Sometimes these lines have two harpoons attached, so that if one misses the whale, another can be ready to take effect, before the creature is beyond their reach. The lance is fixed to a line in a similar manner, by which it may be drawn out of the animal, as it is repeatedly thrust into him, until he is killed by bleeding to death; a process sometimes requiring two or three hours for its completion.

The boats remain beside the dead animal until the ships come to them, for they are generally unable to tow him to the ship, in consequence of his great weight. When brought alongside the vessel, a chain, called the fluke chain, is fastened around his tail, which is towards the bow of the vessel, by which means he is made secure to it. From his carcass are then cut large junks of oily

10*

substance, called blubber, which is from twelve to eighteen inches in thickness, and is the only fleshy part of any value. These junks are hoisted upon deck, and placed in cauldron kettles, that the oil may be tried and pressed from them ; after which, the refuse is thrown upon the fire and used for fuel.

There are five different kinds of whale : the sperm, the right, the humpback, the finback, and the sulphur bottom, of which but three are much caught, the sperm, the right and the humpback. The first is found in warm climates, the last in temperate, but the right in cold. Two men are generally placed aloft as " lookouts," while the ship is cruising for whales, which may often be seen at a distance of two miles, usually by their spouting, which is sometimes repeated as often as every half minute. The whale can neither stay long above nor below the water, without changing.

When the whale is discovered, the signal is given to the captain, or the officer upon the deck watch, in the following manner: The man aloft says, " There she blows." The officer inquires " Where away ?" " Two points of the weather beam, sir," is the reply, or whatever direction the animal may be. This signal is repeated every time the whale spouts, until the officer goes aloft, to determine of what kind the animal is.

Part of the crew are always on the watch, while the others are asleep below. Orders are now given to call all hands on deck, which being done, each boat's crew stations itself by its boat, until orders are given for lowering them away. When within reach of the whale, the officer in command gives orders for the harpooner to throw his instrument, which he does until the animal is fastened. The whale can only be killed by lancing him under the fin, which is the work of much skill and practice.

The whale is a monster, terrible in his fury, but harmless when left alone ; able to shiver the boat in atoms by one stroke of his tail, and when in agony roaring like a lion in the forest. Hence the officer in the boat should have as much skill in the art of whaling, as a military commander in the art of warfare, since the safety of the crew rests with him.

CHAP. XVII.

AFTER leaving Fayal, we sailed for St. Paul's Island, stopping a short time at the Cape de Verdes, where right whales were said to be numerous. We had pleasant weather for about three weeks.

One day, while standing upon the deck, looking upon the broad expanse of waters spread out around me, and meditating upon the works of the Omnipotent and Omniscient Deity, my soul was suddenly so filled with the Holy Ghost, that I exclaimed aloud, " Glory to God and the Lamb forever!" I continued in this strain until captain Luce, coming unexpectedly behind me, asked what was the matter with me? I told him my soul had caught new fire from the burning altar of God, until I felt happy, soul and body.

Directly he commenced cracking jokes at me, but I soon left his presence and returned to the cabin, where I could be, for a while, alone, and where I could obtain spiritual strength to enable me to stand before wicked men.   There is no better time to pray, than when God is ready to answer ; when he stands knocking at the door of our hearts, pleading for entrance.   He works upon our right hand and our left, and we perceive him not.

The captain, being in a very pleasant mood, one day, came into the cabin, and asked me if I ever prayed for him ? to which I replied I did. " Do you think that your prayer is answered ?" he asked, " for I don't. I don't think they ascend higher than the foreyard."   I told him that bread cast upon the waters, was sometimes found and gathered after many days.   He laughingly asked me if I prayed that the ship might get a load of oil?   I told him I always prayed for the blessing of God on the ship in general.   He said if he had to go home without a load of oil, which he expected to do, that he should call me a hypocrite.

While he was talking, the man on the lookout cried out, " There she blows," upon which he ran upon deck, and found there were four whales in sight, not more than three-fourths of a mile distant.   The mate, who was be-low, springing from his bed, said, " Steward, will you go in my boat ?"   I replied I would.   " Then," said he, " Stand by the boat."

The boats being lowered, we started for the whales. The mate rushed among them, and fastened one ; the captain soon followed, and fastened another ; and at last, the second mate to another! They all furnished 239 bbls. of oil. This was a day of rejoicing for all hands, as we had not seen a whale before for more than five weeks. The mate, who had before been my enemy, now became my friend, and during the remainder of the voyage treated me like a man.

On our way to the Dutch Banks, whither the captain concluded to go, because of the abundance of whales there, we caught two, and fastened upon a third, which, however, got loose. When we arrived at the Banks, we found plenty of whales, and many vessels there for the purpose of taking them; but which, in consequence of stormy weather, had hitherto been unsuccessful, and for the same reason we only took three.

For about three weeks the storm raged most furiously, the wind became a hurricane, the waves rolled and dashed mountain high, sweeping our boats from their hangings, and dashing them in pieces; while the sun was hid by dark and portentuous clouds.

All hands looked upon the captain as their deliverer, while he stood looking at the clouds, seemingly with deprecating vengeance. But it was the work of our God, whom the winds obey, and to whom the sea does homage. Well might the Scripture say, "He has his ways in the whirlwinds, and his paths are known to the mighty deep." He looks, and the fearfully threatening clouds hide their deformed faces; He speaks, and the winds hushed in profound silence; He commands, and the lofty billows lowly bow their heads.

The storm being over, we sailed for St. Pauls, where

we took several whales; but had two of our boats stove to pieces, in encounters with them. The Captain and first mate's boats were frequently injured in this way; but the second mate generally kept in the background until the danger and bustle were passed. Here I again had time to reflect upon past blessings; while calmness prevails, the mariner should prepare for a storm; for the storm, which gathers slowly, accumulates more fury than a sudden, transient blast.

> " Whene'er becalmed I lie,
>   And storms forbear to toss;
>   Be thou, dear Lord, still nigh,
>   Lest I should suffer loss:
> For more the treacherous calm I dread,
> Than tempest, bursting overhead."

Captain Luce was a good seaman and captain, and a man of reliable judgment. He would allow no swearing on board his vessel; he looked upon the sailors as his children, and they in turn regarded him with affectionate esteem. The mate was a man of quick passions, easily excited, but as easily calmed.

He one night entered the cabin, where I was, while I was singing one of the songs of Zion, and being in a melancholy mood, he asked me to sing for him; with which request I gladly complied, by commencing a new song, which I had recently learned in Philadelphia. He instantly stopped me, saying he did not wish to hear any new hymn, but some old and substantial one; upon which I sang the following:

"Before Jehovah's awful throne,
Ye nations bow with sacred awe;
Know that the Lord is God alone:
He can create and he destroy.

His sovereign power, without our aid,
Made us of clay, and formed us men;
And when, like wandering sheep, we strayed,
He brought us to his fold again.

Wide as the world is his command,
Vast as eternity his love;
Firm as a rock his truth shall stand,
When rolling years shall cease to move."

While I was singing, tears came into his eyes, and when I ceased, he exclaimed, "Oh! steward, had I the religion which I think you have, I would not part with it for all the world!" This was a very unexpected compliment to me, from a man in so high a station, and encouraged me to pray on and hope continually.

After the whaling season at St. Pauls was ended, we went to the Crowsett Island, where it was very cold, and where the fogs continued a long time, without intermission. We had good success in whaling there, but the weather was so unfavorable, that the hands soon became disabled by scurvey, to that degree that we were obliged to put into port sooner than the captain had intended. So we sailed towards Madagascar, where one remarkable circumstance occurred.

We had a sailor on board named Smith, who told me the reason for his coming on this voyage, was, that being in company with some firemen, in Brooklyn, who had committed a crime in which he was implicated, he had adopted this as the best means of eluding the vigilance of the officers, who were in pursuit of him, and who had taken some of the company.

I told him that he could not so easily escape from God, that the remembrance of his crime would still pursue him, and that unless he repented, he must expect severe punishment, both here and hereafter: to all which he only replied by laughing in my face.

Soon after this conversation a whale was seen, and Smith belonged to one of the boats sent in pursuit. The animal was harpooned, but stove the boat, and broke loose. In the encounter, Smith came near losing his life. When they returned, I thought it a good time to again refresh his memory, in reference to his crime. While the fright lasted, he seemed somewhat penitent, but the feeling soon passed away, like the fleeting time.

Not long after, a similar circumstance happened to him, which was as soon forgotten. But a repetition of them, made him afraid to go in the boat, so he excused himself to the captain, upon the plea that he had cut his finger and could not row; whereupon the mate, to whose boat he belonged, gladly took me in his place; when we, in a short time, captured four whales, with no accident.

Just before we left this Island, another whale was seen, when the captain ordered Smith to go in his usual place, notwithstanding he attempted, as usual, to excuse himself, upon the ground of his inability to row: to all which the captain turned a deaf ear. They soon came up with the whale and harpooned him, when he stove the boat all in pieces, throwing the crew all into the sea, where they were struggling for their lives, by clinging to pieces of wreck or whatever else they could reach. The other boats at the time, were at a great distance from this scene, one of them being already fastened to another whale.

Smith strove manfully to keep himself above water, until finding his strength failing, he made for a piece of the wreck, on which were already three persons, but which could not sustain a fourth; so those first in possession of the frail support, thinking three lives of more consequence than one, as the only means of self-preservation, pushed Smith off into the deep, and would not permit him to grasp their piece of wreck.

The poor fellow was for a time quite at a loss what course to pursue, but time pressed, his strength was fast failing, and he must make some effort, even though he perish in the attempt, it could be no worse, since he must surely perish if he remained where he was. The whale was then lying quietly upon the water, near by. Quick as thought Smith conceived the hazardous plan of saving himself, by clinging to that enemy, which he had just been using all his power and skill to destroy, and as quickly grasped the line attached to the harpoon, which was still sticking in the whale, and by its help climbed upon his back, where, holding by the handle of the harpoon, he rested securely until a boat came and took him off! Then was the moment when Smith, in the agony, and from the depths of his heart, cried, " Lord save, or I perish !" and Heaven heard the rebel's prayer, and held that mighty leviathan, and made him the means of

11

his persecutor's preservation! For as soon as Smith was taken off his back, he went down and came up again a .half mile distant.

This terrible fright lasted Smith nearly two weeks, during which I again reminded him of his crime, and of his wanderings from the path of rectitude. I strove to make him realize how wonderfully the Lord had preserved his life, and how mercifully He had dealt with him; to all which Smith replied, by promising that henceforth he would serve the Lord better.

We reached Madagascar, which is an African island, and of immense dimensions I am told, about the first of May; but I cannot give my readers a geographical description of it, as I only went about five miles inland; nor need I, for it might weary their patience, while to speak of some of the manners and customs of the inhabitants, might mantle with blushes the cheek of morality. The soil is rich, producing in abundance rice, cotton, corn, sugar cane, &c.

The natives are black, with long straight hair, slender forms, and remarkable for their longevity. They are cunning and much disposed to plunder. Their religion is Mahomedan, though they practice many Jewish rites, such as sacrifice and burnt offerings, for which purpose they raise many cattle. They consider the white man a superhuman being, who can hold converse with the Almighty, who will speak to him as He will not to them. One day they stood looking with amazement at the mate, as he was taking the sun's altitude with a quadrant. When he had finished his observations, he offered the in-

strument to several of them, all of whom refused it, saying, God would not talk to them as he did to white
men!

I was much gratified, upon conversing with them, to
learn that they had some faint knowledge of the true and
living God, and believed Mahomet was only a mediator
between God and man. A woman, who I least expected
would possess any such knowledge, gave me to understand that she believed God dwelt above in the heavens,
and that at some future time he would come to judge the
world.

Wednesday was my day to go on shore, and Thursday
the cook's day. But being one day on shore, I learned
that the following day was one devoted by the natives to
sacrificial offerings, which I would not tell the cook, lest
curiosity should prompt him to go to see them, and thus
deprive me of a chance. So I paid him to stay and do
my cabin work, and let me go on shore again that day.

This offering was to secure the blessing of their Hoker-
barro, or God, on the king and his family. The sacrifice
was performed in this manner: three poles, 15 or 20
feet in length, with shorter ones lying across them, were
placed three feet above the ground. When this was done,
the sacrificial bullock was brought to look upon it, after
which he was killed, his blood caught in a calabash, or
gourd, for a separate offering, and his flesh cut in pieces
and laid upon the poles, under which a fire was kindled,
around which the natives danced, clapping their hands
while it was burning, the whole performance being
accompanied by numerous ceremonies. Tho sacrifice

ends with the sunset, but as my duty required my attendance on shipboard before that time, I did not witness its conclusion.

We remained in Madagascar three weeks to repair the ship, which was damaged at sea. While lying in port four of the crew escaped, and were concealed on shore by the natives ; who afterwards came and betrayed them to the captain for a price. The mate, with a boat's crew of Portuguese, was sent for them, with whom they not only refused to return, but severely cut and bruised them. Afterwards the captain, with the captains of five other vessels, then lying in port, went for them, conducted by the natives, who knew their place of concealment, in a native hut.

When he discovered them, the captain calmly told them he wished them to return with him to their duty on board the vessel, to which they readily gave their assent, saying they would have gone before had he sent Americans for them, but that they would not willingly submit to be fettered by Portuguese.

When they reached the ship, they were placed in irons, and put upon criminal's allowance until the next morning, when it was expected they would receive their deserved punishment. Our captain did not wish to flog them, as he thought he could inflict some other punishment which would prove more salutary and efficacious ; but, being pressingly urged by captain Burton, of the ship Sally Ann, and others, to do so, he finally flogged three of them, among whom was Smith ; while one, who was not concerned in resisting the Portuguese, was suffered to go without his flogging. But before we were ready to leave Madagascar, this very man again escaped from the vessel, by lying upon a plank and paddling himself along with his hands, he having previously arranged with the crew of the ship to which he was going, to receive him on board and conceal him, which they did, until she was ready to sail for New London, whither she was bound, loaded with oil.

CHAP. XVIII.

WE cruised around the coast of Africa for whales, but finding none, put into the port of Johanna, where we again met the ship Sally Ann, captain Burton, who had the reputation of being a very cruel man.

While lying in port, six or seven of his men, taking with them provisions, a compass, quadrant, chart, nautical almanac, spy glass, and other useful implements of navigation, one morning before daylight, took a boat and made off, intending to go to Mohilla, one of the Comoro Islands, about ten miles from Johanna. But before they were out of sight, they were discovered from the ship.

Now, there is a reef of rocks running about one and a half miles out to sea, from the port of Johanna, which are, at all times, very dangerous, in consequence of the heavy seas which are constantly breaking over them. When captain Burton discovered and gave chase to his deserting crew, they ran at once among these reefs, and

11*

thus escaped, he not daring to follow them, but returning to his ship much fatigued and exasperated.

It seemed that the Johannicans and Mohillans had been at war with each other, and consequently no intercourse was permitted between the islands. Captain Burton offered the Johanna king a large reward, if he would catch his runaways, and deliver them up to him when he returned from a short cruise, which he was now obliged to make, and from which he should return in about three weeks. But the king, fearing to approach the shores of his enemy's island, only cruised about his own, and of course with no success ; so he finally gave up the search, and the ship was obliged to put out to sea without them, though the captain swore he would have them, if they went to hell!

Five days afterwards they discovered a sperm whale, after which they immediately gave chase. He went down and finally came up very near the captain's boat, when he gave orders to harpoon him, which the boatsteerer immediately did, and fastened him. The captain then went forward to lance him, when the whale struck him so violent a blow with his tail, as to break both his legs, without injuring another person. He was taken directly to Johanna, but there being no surgeon there, he was obliged to remain in this painful situation, until an English vessel, having one on board, came into port. But by this time his limbs were so badly swollen, that one of them could not be properly set, so he was taken to Cape Town, from whence he was sent to America. Three of his runaway crew were taken on board a French vessel, nearly in a state of starvation, while the rest actually perished.

We lay in this port about a week. It is a very ancient town, the houses of one story, mostly built of stone, and seldom having any windows. The inhabitants are Arabs, Malays and Africans. They are of a light brown complexion, and have regular features. Their religion is Mahomedan, the rites of which they scrupulously observe. They are exceedingly jealous of their females, insomuch that they will not permit them to speak to any man, out of their own family circle. They wear sad countenances, but are very hospitable. They have large and splendidly decorated temples, the floors of which are covered with striped matting, of their own manufacture.

One of the natives, who seemed a man of some influence and high moral standing, one day invited me to visit, with him, one of these temples; which invitation I gladly accepted. When we reached the door, my conductor stopped to speak to a person who I supposed was a priest, as he sat by a table on which lay a book and many papers, from which he was reading in a tuneful voice. A stone trough was standing beside the church.

I bolted at once into the temple, without hesitation, but was as soon brought back and told that I had defiled it, in consequence of not purifying myself before entering. The priest seemed very much offended, but led me to the trough, in which was a constantly changing supply of clean, fresh water, and bade me wash my hands and feet before entering.

I was told that my sacrilegious entrance, unpurified, would oblige them to perform an extra sacrifice, by way

of atonement. I regretted much that I had unwittingly
been the cause of so much trouble, and thought an ac-
knowledgment a sufficient sacrifice, but I was mistaken.

After being properly prepared, I was allowed to enter
and remain during their service. I was astonished at
the reverence and humility with which they approached
the throne of grace, for they fell flat upon their faces.

Many things might be said concerning the manners
and customs prevalent on this Island, as also concerning
its towns ; but my business is to describe my voyage to
the Indian Ocean, to which I will now return.

We left this Island, and sailed in the direction of New
Zealand, near which we cruised five weeks, taking several
whales in the time. Four other vessels were in company
with us here, each of which went in for himself, taking
whales.

During one of our whaling adventures, I unwillingly
consented to accompany the mate, at his request. I at-
tributed most of the accidents to his carelessness ; notwithstanding, he was called a skillful whaleman, therefore I did not like to go with him. He would rush to
attack a whale, like a restless horse to battle, harpooning
him without any regard to order or formality, lest some
other boat should secure him first. We here took three
whales in one week.

We one day fell in with a ship from Sag Harbor, having on board the dead bodies of two men, the captain of
which came on board the Milwood, one beautiful Sabbath
morning, when the sea was as smooth as glass, to ask
our captain and such of the crew as chose to accompany

him, to go on board his ship and attend their funeral.

I went and witnessed what is, probably, one of the most solemn and affecting of scenes,—a burial at sea. All who witnessed it were affected with sadness. When all was ready for the final ceremony, the bodies were taken to the waist gangway, where they were lashed upon boards, lying upon their backs, with heavy bags of sand attached to their feet, after which they were committed to the waves, and instantly sank into the vast deep. Captain Luce performed the religious services with great solemnity.

After crusing in these seas about two months, we put into a harbor on New Zealand, where we stayed one week, and then went to New Holland for the cure of the scurvy, with which the sailors were badly afflicted, in consequence of having been so long exposed to an atmosphere loaded with saline vapors, and of being so long fed upon salted food. Eating raw potatoes is considered by some an excellent remedy for this disease, which commences with an irruption of the skin, and ends in putrefaction, if not arrested in season to prevent.

Another remedy, and one to which our sailors were subjected, is reckoned very good, namely : to bury the patient in the ground, all but his head, for a while. After the diseased ones had thus been cured, we cruised for a long time with no success, and finally returned to the Crowsett Islands ; but even here were unsuccessful.

We had now been at sea over two years, and had completed our cargo, all save 50 bbls., when our captain decided to cruise towards home, keeping up a sharp look-

out, until we were beyond the whaling ground. This
decision filled me with joy, for I yearned to see my long
unseen family.

The captain said to me one day, when we had been
sometime homeward bound, "Steward, I thought you
promised us a full cargo to return with, which you see
we have not got; so I must 'think you a hypocrite!" I
told him I still believed my prayers would be answered,
and that we should yet have a full cargo.

About two weeks after this, while the ship, with all her
canvas spread, and with a fair wind, was running after
the rate of nine knots an hour, the man aloft saw two
whales in the distance. The captain had offered ten dollars for a whale that would furnish 50 bbls. of oil, and
each man was desirous of winning the prize. Preparations were soon made to give chase to the whales, who
were still at a considerable distance from the ship.

The mate's boat soon fastened one whale, but while
the captain was striving to fasten the other, he stove the
boat and tumbled the crew into the water. The mate's
crew, however, after killing their whale, took after this,
and finally secured him, while the second mate's boat
picked up the almost despairing crew. The two whales
filled 150 bbls. with oil, so that there was not place in
the ship to stow it, without throwing over some of the
provisions to make room. We then went into Soldonna
for refreshment, and while there lost four of our crew
by desertion.

We next stopped at St. Helena, which renowned place
I was very glad to see, and took occasion to visit the res-

idence and tomb of the Emperor Napoleon. But I discovered nothing very remarkable at either place, therefore will not weary my readers with unimportant description. After one week's stay we left St. Helena for the American coast.

About three days out from this island, we spoke a ship, recently from home, by which the captain learned that since he left home his wife had given birth to a son. This filled him with joy, and made him so anxious to reach home, that he ordered the mate to put the ship under all the sail which she would bear.

The wind blew so furiously that it sometimes seemed as if the sails must all be carried away; but like a gallant bark, the ship safely outrode the whole, and arrived at New Bedford. No pilot being in sight, we had to fire twenty rounds from the cannon as a signal, before we could raise one. At last, however, to our great joy, a pilot boat hove in sight, dancing over the waves, when shouts were heard, " O, sir, we shall soon get into harbor!" Then the joyful hymn was sung:—

" By faith I see the land,
  The port of endless rest;
 My soul, each sail expand,
  And fly to Jesus' breast.
 Oh! may I gain that heavenly shore,
 Where winds and waves disturb no more."

But our singing was soon turned into sighing, our joy into sadness, for our pilot, being unacquainted with the New Bedford channel, could only take us in sight of the city, where we were left nearly two days to brood over our bitter disappointment.

How often do professed ministers of the Christian Church pretend to lead the anxious soul to the haven of eternal rest, when they are themselves ignorant of the way, and of course leave him in the gulf of despair to mourn his sad disappointment. But the right pilot came at last and took us into New Bedford, and Oh, what joy filled my soul, when I was once more permitted to enter the congregation of the righteous, and to hear the sound of the Gospel Trumpet.

But my bliss was not complete, for I had a family in Philadelphia, whom I must hasten to see, that they might participate in my joy, and unite with me in praises to God for my safe preservation through so long a voyage; so, as soon as I received my wages, I left New Bedford. Before I left, the captain and mate both called to see me, the former giving me ten, and the latter five dollars, telling me to live faithful until death, and asking me to pray for them, which I promised to do, then bade them farewell, and left for Philadelphia.

CHAP. XIX.

WHILE at sea and learning the uses of the various nautical instruments, I also studied their spiritual application, for nothing else so much resembles the passage of a Christian from earth to glory, as a gallant ship under full sail for some distant port. The parallel between ships and souls, of course does not extend to their original structure or nature, since one is mere inert matter, fashioned by human skill, visible and perishable; while the other is immortal, invisible, and the direct handiwork of God.

Simplicity of nature must ever insure immortality under a government where the annihilation of created beings is impossible. Yet numerous are the circumstances in which the parallel will hold, and where the propriety of the metaphor is apparent. Let us contemplate some few of these for a moment, for time would fail us to review the curious machine in all its parts, and speak of its accommodating and beautiful comparison with the faculties of a rational soul; or to the grace of one regenerated and sanctified by the spirit of God.

Pleasant and entertaining as it might be, to consider how this metaphorical ship uses conscience for its helm, the understanding for its rudder, judgment and reason for its masts, its affections for sails; how education stands in the place of carving and gilding; how the passions represent too full sails, thus producing danger from foundering; how pride represents the too taut rigging; how assumed professions represent deceptive and ruinous false colors; yet, we must necessarily waive all such considerations.

Still, we must pause to admire the excellence of the model of this work of God, as much the highest of all this lower creation, as a ship is superior to every other work of human art. Nor can any words sufficiently deplore that misfortune by which, on its first being launched upon the ocean of life, this noble vessel was dashed on the rocks of presumption, and thus, in an unlucky moment, condemned and cast away utterly unfit for service.

How poor a pilot is man, even with his highest knowledge and ability, and how unfit to take his soul into his own keeping. And how magnanimous the grace of the generous Owner, who, instead of destroying that insignificant wreck, as might have been expected, was pleased to repair the ruins ; notwithstanding he was well aware it would be a work of more difficulty and labor, than to construct an entirely new one, which could have been done by a word ; while to restore the old wreck, would cost the greatest treasure in heaven, the life of the great owner and builder's only begotten and well beloved son ! Oh, amazing love ! that could so highly value things so worthless ; things only fitted to be cast into the den of wild and furious beasts, or the dreary abóde of unclean birds !

From the Omnipotent Power and Infinite Skill of the divine undertaker of the work, as well as the invaluable price given to defray the expenses, reason would immediately conclude, that in rebuilding this moral and spiritual structure, which was shipwrecked in Adam, but redeemed in Christ, no pains would be spared, nor anything omitted, which would be necessary to complete the work on which Jehovah's heart was set, and to make the second structure more glorious than the first.

Nor was the conclusion unfounded, for every material was purchased by the blood of the Son of God, and laid in bountifully by the gracious owner. Every piece is

hewn by the law in the work of conviction ; every facul-
ty purged from sin and guilt by the great atonement, received by faith in Christ Jesus ; every plank bent by the
fire of divine love, all fitted to their places by the invinci-
ble energy of sovereign grace, and the structure is completed according to the model prepared in the council of
peace, and published in the gospel, which divine illumination is made visible to the mental eye, through which
it is received into the heart, and leaves its impress there.
Destined for a voyage of vast importance, in seas beset with dangers and perils, this new vessel will find
nothing more needful than a strong and sound bottom.

If faith is not genuine and enduring; if those principles typified by the planks and timbers of a ship, be rot-
ten or unsound at heart, not consistent with each other,
and not shaped so as to lie compactly ; or if each is not
well secured by bolts of the endurable metal of eternal
truth from the mine of divine revelation ; if all is not carefully caulked with the powerful cement of unfailing love
and redeeming blood ; in a word, if Christ is not the sole
foundation, and his righteousness the grand security,
then on the slightest trial, the seams open, the vessel
bilges, and every soul on board is lost.

From the hour of active conversion, the redeemed soul
is launched upon the deep, and moves in a new element.
As she proceeds onward, and greater depths surround
her, the amazing wonders of divine counsel appear more
manifest, which had hitherto been unknown and un-
fathomed by any human line ; the latent corruptions
within its own recesses appear more terrible as farther

explored, and every new glimpse still more affrights and humbles; while the mysterious and inexplicable depths of divine Providence, with its mercies, judgments, and deliverances also rise to view.

She floats on an ocean of trouble, where temptations inflame the appetite, and weaken good resolutions, as worms pierce through and destroy the bottom of a vessel. Trials follow each other, as wave succeeds wave; nor should we feel ourselves alone, nor more sorely tempted than others, in this, since it is the experience of every one who floats upon life's ocean billows. When our sorrows are mitigated, our thankfulness should increase; and when the clouds of grief become thicker and darker, it should wean us more effectually from earthly things, and kindle within us a more ardent desire for heavenly things.

Nor should the Christian repine at his afflictions, for he could not well do without them, since no means is more effectual to weaken the force of inate sin, or to wean him from his earthly idols, even as the heat of a furnace keeps the seething metal in commotion, while it separates and drives off the dross; or the unceasing rolling of the restless ocean, which, I am told serves to keep its waters pure. In contemplating the fickleness of this uncertain world, let us not fail to draw instruction therefrom.

Bound, as she is, to take a voyage on this restless, troubled ocean, the spiritual ship must not only be furnished with rigging suited to such a bottom as I have described, but she must also be provided with all necessary nautical instruments before she can safely put to sea ; and oh, how carefully has her gracious owner been, that all her wants should be supplied.

An invariable and unfailing compass is furnished by the Sacred Scriptures, whose direction may be safely followed in the darkest night. The divine illumination will serve as a quadrant by which the Christian may discover his own latitude, and his position in regard to the path of rectitude and duty ; but in vain will the most experienced seaman attempt to do this, unless his sun shines, and his horizon is clear.

How often, by persuading men to neglect the use of this quadrant, and thereby lose their true situation, has satan decoyed men to accept his pilotage, and trust to his skill, until he had led them clear out of the right course, to the very mouth of the gulf of despondency, among rocks and quicksands on all sides.

Through the spy glass of faith, the Christian may discover his faithful starry guides, although the heavens be shrouded in clouds ; or may descry the approaching enemy, and avoid him ; or may discover the far off haven of security. In the same manner self-examination may supply to the believing soul a line and lead, whereby to sound the waters, discover the way, and learn his distance, both from the port of departure and that to which he is bound.

A longing to arrive at a blessed end of the voyage, serves as an hour glass, by which he may mark the swiftly passing hours, and so reckon his time, that he may be able to give a correct account of it to the great ship owner ; especially as he is sensible that not one hour can

12*

pass unremarked.   This glass also admonishes him to set
the watch at the exact minute, lest the steersman sleep
at his helm, the hands slacken their diligence in duty,
the vessel lose its way, or storms or enemies come unawares and find it unprepared.   Precious moments, how
swiftly they fly, every wave of the wing hastening us onward to eternity.   Oh, that Christians would more carefully note their falling sands, and renew their watch
more frequently.   Failing to do this, caused David's pen-
itential agony, and Peter's bitter tears of anguish.

To often try the pump is no less necessary than to
change the watch, for which purpose is given sincere re-
pentance, such as sinks to the bottom of the heart, search-
es out every lust and evil desire, brings it to the surface,
and casts it out, as does the pump-rod the stagnant blige-
water, which, if allowed to remain, would finally sink the
vessel.

On the ocean of life, where we are constantly meeting
vessels, steering in every possible direction, would that
Christians would show the same courtesy and kindness
to each other, that seamen of every nation and under all
colors, do.   Then, with what true interest would they
hail each other, with what courtesy answer when asked
where they were bound, and with what good wishes send
them on their way to their place of destination.   With
what truthfulness would they give an account of their
voyage, of their adventures, of their cargo, and also of
their reasons for the hope that is within them, with fear
and meekness ; so that believers might in this way become comforters, helpers, and directors to each other.

And that they might be thoroughly furnished for so good a work, their gracious owner has put on board a silver trumpet, whose sound is never false nor unreliable. I mean the Gospel, which brings glad tidings to all within sound of its voice, and speaks in a language which people of all nations can understand. In this language all may converse together, however much they may differ in other things ; and all imbued with its spirit will gladly bear each other company, and hold communion together, in so far as time and circumstances will allow.

Defensive arms, also, are necessary for the safety of the voyage, and accordingly, see how completely the thoughtful owner has equipped the ship at his own expense. A full inventory of the armory may be found recorded in Ephsians, 6 : 14—18.

But all else would fail were a cable and anchor wanting, both which are supplied, the one by hope, the other by faith. Thus completed and supplied with every necessary, the good ship takes in her lading. The various gifts and graces of the Holy Ghost, together with the hopes and comforts arising from their exercise; the bracelets, the signets, and stuffs, the evidences and manifestations of the divine favor ; goodly pearls selected from the treasury of unsearchable riches in Christ Jesus, all the special furniture, privileges, enjoyments, and experiences of the true believer, purchased for him by the blood of his dying Redeemer, are now put on board by orders of the Spirit of Sanctification : while, at the same time, every needful store is furnished by the precious promises and glorious truths of the gospel, of which a

spirit of faith and prayer keeps the key, from whence
the believer may daily draw and drink of the waters of
Life ; and upon which he may fare sumptuously every
day.

Bound for the port of endless rest, the soul thus equipped receives sailing orders from the inspired oracles,
which, at the same time, commands her to forsake all, to
deny herself, to take up the cross, and to follow the Lamb
whithersoever he goeth. If sincerely desirous to proceed, she will be very careful to have all things in readiness, and all hands in waiting for a favorable wind, without which the truest helm or the ablest steersman will be
of no avail.   Oh, Christian friends, were we but as earnest for the port of glory, as the mariner is for some
earthly port, we should not often be found loitering or off
our duty.   Our prayers would ascend with every breath,
that the heavenly gale would spring up, and awake the
church from her lethargic slumbers.

How carefully then should we accompany our prayers
with watching, heedfully marking every changeful appearance of the sky. How eagerly should we seize the
first favorable moment, when the long wished for opportunity of sailing was in our power. Eager for departure,
we would not willingly lose one fair breeze, knowing that
without this all previous preparations were fruitless. Nor
must the fairest gale entice us to sea without the heavenly pilot ; for without thee, blessed Jesus, we can do nothing ; to thee we must turn in every difficulty, and upon
thee call in every time of danger. We dare trust no
other at the helm, because no other can safely steer us

past the rocks and quicksands. How kind thy promise, to be with us when passing through deep and dangerous waters. How gracious thy word which engages never to leave nor forsake us. We will confidently leave our feeble vessel entirely to thy guiding care, to shape its course and direct its way ; nor will we dread the greatest danger, with thy hand upon the helm, believing no hidden rock can escape thy penetrating eye, nor any storm or danger surpass thy skill, or counteract thy unbounded power.

The hour arrives, all is in readiness, the pilot gives the signal, the anchor is weighed, and with all sails set, our bark proceeds to sea. What more majestic sight than a gallant ship, under full sail, wafted by a fair gale, proudly cutting her way through the vast deep? And so of the Holy Ghost, spreading every sail, that the kindly gales of the spirit of all grace, may waft it safe to the heavenly port, while the beams of the sun of Righteousness gild and brighten the scene.

Such halcyon days are sometimes vouchsafed to the young convert, just starting on life's new voyage. Oh, how should he improve them while within his reach, by preparing for the coming change! But alas! the treachery of the heart sometimes perverts such favors into occasions of spiritual pride. Then may be seen displayed the colors of mere profession ; the streamers of confidence flying ; the top gallant sails of self-conceit hoisted ; the haughty royals set, and the vessel of self-righteousness mounted loftily on the waves.

Alas! how many have been thus wrecked in a vainglorious moment; and life has paid the forfeit of such insolence of heart, disdaining to proportion the sail to the ballast. Such an abuse of mercy could not escape the all-penetrating eye. The golden season suddenly expires, and is succeeded by a dead calm. The poor self-admirer lays his head in the lap of some bewitching Delilah, who lulls him to sleep with her siren songs.

Now all the Christian graces lie dormant; all precepts, ordinances and means are lost on a person so facinated; while the rolling billows serve only to rock him into a deeper sleep. With no guide at the helm, such a ship gains nothing in her course. Could conscience only gain a hearing, all hands would quickly be roused to prepare for the coming storm; the leisure of the threatening calm would not be consumed in slothfulness.

Instead of inactivity and delay, when dangers threaten, the real, active believer is on the alert. While becalmed, he is examining his stores and cargo, patching his sails, and splicing his rigging. Spy glass in hand, he is searching for a clear coast. His journal is revised and his reckoning adjusted, his quadrant applied and his observations compared. Did we but judiciously employ the hour of tranquility, we should have little to fear from tempests.

But while all hands are negligently folded in security, and thoughtlessness fills the dreams of all, the change comes, contrary winds arise, obstacles spring up, difficulties beset the way, and all where least expected. Now we are forced by adversity to lower those sails, which, in the season of sunshine we hoisted, just to gain applause.

Like Babylon, which, in its pride, vainly exalted itself, and was finally humbled. Dan. 5: 20. Ob. 1: 3.

But notwithstanding adverse winds may blow, the faithful mariner will not haul in all sail, and lash the helm, thus leaving his vessel to the sport of fate. On the contrary, he will lose no chance of taking advantage of every fair breeze, to do which he will trim his sails to the wind, laying his course as near as possible, even though he cannot lay it direct. With the Bible in his hand for his compass, he steers his way, going not to the conclaves of councils, nor to the decrees of earthly potentates for his creed or the rule of his duty.

Disdaining to be the slave of popularity, he will neither embrace opinions because of their fashionableness, nor trim his principles to suit the times, nor yet follow the multitude to do evil. By experience he is taught to trust no mere professions, but like the panting slave fleeing from the bondman's chains and dungeon, he is suspicious of even a brother fugitive, who says he is travelling the same road, lest he should be betrayed. For freedom, like eternal life, is precious, and a true man will risk every power of body or mind to escape the snares of satan, and secure an everlasting rest at the right hand of God.

THE END.

WS - #0146 - 121222 - C0 - 229/152/8 - PB - 9781331804390 - Gloss Lamination